TOUCHING HUNGER

STORIES & POEMS

PETER SANFORD KAHRMANN

Sanford
November 2022

For my sister, Rebecca Jill Kahrmann.

1958-2021

Table of Contents

Patterns On Canvas

Winter.

Nine o'clock Saturday morning. Wind-driven mean cold washed over the streets of Pearl River. Winston's Newsstand opened at five a.m. Seven days a week Steven Winston opens the shop promptly at five a.m. Steven is twenty-six. He is the fourth-generation owner. His great-great-grandfather, Marcus Winston, opened in 1918, after the war to end all wars.

Like most places in life, things you could really count on were often in short supply. However, residents of Pearl River could count on Winston's Newsstand.

Winston's Newsstand had the best coffee in town. Common knowledge. Marcus Winston used to say: "Life is tough enough. No one should be shorted on a good cup of coffee."

No one argued.

Steven Winston was a stocky five six, dark chocolate eyes. Wore glasses, a reality he hated. He'd been next in line to run the family store, another reality he hated. It wasn't that he hated the customers or his family or the store. What he hated was being stuck in Pearl River.

The only good thing about living in Pearl River was he was in love with Kitty Delia, and she lived in Pearl River. He'd been in love with Kitty Delia since kindergarten. She was good enough to tolerate him back then. Kitty, with the famous Delia chestnut brown hair, then and now past her shoulders: thick, shiny, glorious waves. Good enough to eat. Her eyes dark, deep-set, glistening. Chocolate brown.

Her face a soft oval, her lips, further evidence Michelangelo had ample reason to sculpt the human form. Now, at twenty-six, she was as beautiful as ever. More so in Steven's eyes.

They had never been an item.

But toleration turned to a real friendship after Kitty's house caught fire. Kitty was seventeen and suffered third-degree burns on her left arm. Many neighborhood boys who'd nearly begged for the chance to go out with her disappeared, some casting petals of pitiable expressions in their wake.

Not so Steven Winston.

He really did love her and care about her and made a point of visiting her in the hospital and when she was recovering at home.

The first time she put on a sleeveless dress after the fire, exposing her badly scarred arm, she called Steven and asked him to please come over. When he got there, she showed him her arm and asked him how she looked.

"Don't lie to me, Steven. Tell me the truth."

And he did. He told her the truth. "You look beautiful, Kitty." He meant it.

"People are going to stare."

"The hell with them. Let'm stare. Hell, if those burn patterns were on canvas someone would call it a great abstract painting about the storms of life and pay millions for it!"

She laughed. "You know, you're right." She looked at her arm and said: "I name thee, Pompeii."

Steven smiled. "You're beautiful, Kitty."

The Fare

A brief flicker of shadow crossed her face as she got into the cab. She was pale and thin. She was thirty-five years old and looked older. Her hair was shoulder length, the color of straw. He could not see her eyes in the mirror. She was looking down at her lap, looking for something it seemed.

"Where to?" he asked, hand poised to hit the meter.

"How much time you have?" She was still looking down. "I'd like to ride around a while, see some places, if you don't mind."

"It's your cab, lady. It's a little after eight, my shift's two hours old and twelve hours long. My day's just beginning, I've got plenty of time."

"I'm a great fan of time," she said, looking at him in the mirror and smiling. Her smile brought her slate-gray eyes to life.

He started the meter. "Where to?"

Two hours earlier, she'd faced herself in the bathroom mirror. I look a mess, she thought, once more pushing her hair back with frail hands. She would not be coming back to this second-floor apartment. She accepted this as much as anyone can accept the end of home. Nine years she'd lived here. It occurred to her that over the last two years she'd grown remarkably adept at accepting things, despite herself really. She'd never been one to accept things with any great degree of comfort. Her father used to call her, his little challenger, because she always demanded explanations, reasons, proof, evidence thank you very much. But now, walking through the rooms, all empty save for a sturdy old couch covered in a worn floral-patterned sheet she'd bought years ago at a store long forgotten, her eyes grew thick and wet with sadness.

She'd had second thoughts about leaving the couch behind, but now she hoped it would be a welcome find for the new tenants. Mr.

Prescott, her landlord, said the new tenants were a newly married couple and needed a couch. He was sure they would like hers, especially after he'd told them what a lovely person she was, so brave, and oh, what a gifted flute player. Even so, leaving it behind wasn't easy. She couldn't count the number of times she'd sat on the couch with Aunt Sally and talked and laughed for hours on end. Aunt Sally, her best friend ever, who died in her sleep four years ago. Go to sleep, not wake up. The end. Strange. The person who dies never knows it.

So, looking in the mirror thinking so much happened here. Her relationship with Rick, her biggest male disappointment ever. Couldn't keep it in his pants. When she found out about the affair she felt as if she'd been stabbed. On the other end of the emotional spectrum or thereabouts, there was the boisterous joy that filled every room during her younger sister Millie's eighteenth birthday party.

Most prominent of all, however, in this home's memory landscape, were the countless times she'd stood at the window overlooking the courtyard playing her flute. Telemann's Fantasia 1 in A made her think, no, that wasn't it, made her feel the Spring's early-morning bird songs. Bach's Partita in A minor, well, that she could play over and over again without tiring of its delicate beauty, its strength. And then, best of all, were the times she let her fingers and breath fly, sending the notes into the air like dozens upon dozens of audible jewels.

Mr. Market down the hall carried her two suitcases downstairs. Mr. Market, a week away from his eightieth birthday, a retired history teacher, swam a mile every morning at the neighborhood Y. Mr. Market with a head a bit too large for his lanky frame, made to appear all the more so by a bald dome surrounded by a shaggy horseshoe of gray hair whose open end framed the forehead of a kind, leathery, clean-shaven face. He cared very much about his young neighbor, more than once saying, "You're the daughter I never had." When she told him she was moving and why, he wept. He promised to visit her. She knew he would.

This morning he hailed the cab for her and helped the cabby put the suitcases in the trunk. Then he gave her a long gentle hug, their heads rubbing softly against each other as they nodded, their voices choking out goodbyes, and then, she was gone. She did not look back. She was sure Mr. Market was waving goodbye.

He was.

Looking at the cabby in the rearview mirror, she asked, "Can we go to West Street please before it becomes the West Side Highway?"

"You got it."

She settled back in the seat. "When I was a little girl Aunt Sally," here she paused, and had the cabby been able to see her up close, he would have seen tears fill her eyes. "Funny no one is named Sally anymore...it's got such a kind sound to it." She sighed. "We'd drive up and down West Side Highway and look at all the passenger ships. Long gone time ago."

"I wish I'd seen'm."

"The biggest was the Queen Elizabeth, the fastest was the United States. The Cunard Line was the big thing. Aunt Sally took me on a tour of the Queen Elizabeth once. Incredible. She sailed on it after the war."

"World War two?"

She nodded to him in the mirror. "The cabins were beautiful, beautiful wood. There was this little wood door you could open next to the cabin door so you could put your shoes in this cubby hole. When you woke up in the morning and opened the door, there they were, all shined and polished!"

On West Street now he drove slower, letting her look at the piers, the bike paths, the walkways speckled with joggers, couples, and singles of all ages, gay and straight, food stands. No ships.

The cabby didn't hear her whisper, "So long ago."

Mornings in the city always reminded her of black and white movies, the streets and buildings varying tones of grays, blacks, whites, browns, very little color. Sometimes a walker or jogger wearing a brightly colored exercise suit seemed to jolt the image. Out of place. Alien to the landscape. Their bright colors nothing more than rude interruptions of the city's muscular grays.

She began coughing. A deep wet guttural cough wracked her body. In moments, her face glistened with sweat.

The cabby, furrow-browed with genuine concern, looked at her in the mirror. "You okay, lady?"

She continued coughing for a few moments, waving his question away soft-wristed, hand flapping. She'd grown pale. He said: "You know the city passed this law says you can't die in a cab. You get jail time if you do."

"So, I've heard," she said, nodding, smiling, the coughing fit ending.

"You sure you're, okay?"

"Yes. Thank you."

For the next two hours, they drove through the city. For reasons unclear to him, the cabby grew comfortable with this pale, hungry-looking woman in his back seat. At one point he asked if she was hungry and she said no, she wasn't, but how would he feel about picking up coffee for the two of them, on her. "I'm not supposed to drink much coffee at all, which, as you might imagine, makes drinking it all the more fun."

A short time later parked on East 23rd Street between First and Second Avenue they drank their coffee.

"You visiting someone? Vacation?"

"Visiting?"

"Your suitcases."

"No. Moving."

"Moving truck taking your other stuff?"

"Yes."

"You're a mystery, lady."

She smiled at him in the mirror. "Thank you. I like that." Looking out the window her expression calm. "Who'd ever thought I'd be a mystery."

"It's not every day someone gets in the cab and says let's drive around and see the sites, 'less of course it's some tourists who want to see some landmarks. St. Patrick's, Empire State, museums. You seem more interested in visiting memories than making them."

"Very perceptive."

"You leaving the area?"

"Yes."

"Now?"

"No. In a few months."

"Where you moving to?"

"I'm not entirely sure, to be perfectly honest."

He chuckled. "See, a mystery lady, like I said... You moving in with family?"

"Most are long gone. My mother died when I was three, then three days later my father went to work and never came home. He was married to the bottle. After he didn't come a few days, my brother Frank, he was just ten, put me on the back of his bike and biked us more than twenty miles to Aunt Sally and Uncle Nick's house. They took us in. Neither of them - Nick was my mother's brother, not my father's - was surprised Dad disappeared. I'll never forget. It was late fall, most of the leaves were off the trees. You know that time when winter begins sneaking into the air? It rained that morning and the air smelled delicious. Always does when the leaves are fresh on the ground. Frank helped me pack some clothes into a pink pillowcase, told me to hold on tight when we got on his bike, a Huffy, had to weigh a thousand pounds, and off we went. I don't think he stopped peddling till we got there."

"Your brother sounds special."

"They didn't make them any braver than Frank. Died in a car accident two years ago, just forty years old."

They were silent for a moment.

"You moving in with someone?"

"Yes," she said, her voice seeming to lift a dark veil between them, a hint of sternness or, perhaps, tension. It was, the cabby knew, telling him to not ask more. He thought he would change the direction of the conversation. "I'm not moving," he said, smiling.

"You live with anyone?"

"By myself. Small place in Brooklyn, studio."

"Where in Brooklyn?"

"Carroll Gardens."

"Nice area, by the Heights."

"It is a nice area. Lot of people don't know Carroll Gardens is named after Charles Carroll. Only Catholic signed the Declaration of Independence." He felt good telling her this because a lot of people thought cabbies were, if not plain stupid, certainly not book lovers like he was. At first it was history books, American history mostly, and biographies. For the last couple of years, he'd been gobbling up novels, short stories. For several months he read all the Cormac McCarthy, Philip Roth, and John Updike he could get his hands on. And for short stories, none better than Bernard Malamud. Then, at the suggestion of his landlord, Mrs. Humphries, a retired English teacher, he tried the classics. Soon he couldn't get enough of them: Dickens, Trollope, Tolstoy, Chekov, Elliot, Balzac, Turgenev, Thackeray, Hardy, Dostoyevsky. What they could do with words! It dawned on him when he was in the middle of Barchester Towers that today's writers, with some exceptions, wrote about experiences. But the writers of old, they were the master story tellers. To his surprise (but not Mrs. Humphries) he found himself contemplating the idea of writing his own stories. At first, the thought struck him as somewhat silly. Though God knows, as a cabby you're never not short on material. The truth was, he didn't have a lot of confidence in himself when he was out from behind the wheel. First of all, he was not highly educated. He'd never been to college, and he had nothing more than a high school equivalency diploma that he didn't even study for. He took the test on a whim, and, to his complete and utter amazement, he passed!

And then, in those quiet secret moments, moments when he allowed himself to think about actually sitting down and writing, he realized he wanted to begin his story with the words, Once upon a time.

Reading had allowed him to discover that certain words, certain phrases, idioms like, Once upon a time, had, through no fault of their own, found themselves fully clothed in the unflattering sinful garment of cliché. Words like darling and sweetheart were, if seen in the light of their actual meaning, beautiful words, magnificent even. But to actually say, Hi darling? That would be like biting full force into a lemon.

Were he to submit something for publishing, beginning with, Once upon a time, he'd be laughed right out of the ballpark. He stopped at a red light and looked in the rearview mirror.

She was crying.

He began looking for some tissue but saw it wasn't necessary. She was already dabbing her eyes with tissue she'd pulled from one of those small packages with a slit down the middle of one side.

"Was it Carroll Gardens?"

She hinted a smile, sighed, and looked out the window. "It's learning something new every day."

"That's a good thing, no?"

She nodded. "Yes. It's a good thing on most days. Do you have dreams?"

"Sometimes," he said, pulling away from the curb and making a left on First Avenue. "Most of the time I don't remember'm. Where to?"

She looked down at a small blue spiral notebook in her lap. "Three-thirty, West 30th. Do you know -?"

"Between eight and ninth," he said, angling the cab west across the avenue. "We'll drop a left on thirty-fourth, go to ninth and cut back on thirtieth."

"Not sleeping dreams. Dreams like wishes. Like the movie bucket list."

Her interest in him was unexpected, pleasantly so. Usually, passengers liked to talk about themselves, their lives, when they talked at all that is. He didn't really mind listening to them. After all, they were paying him, not the other way around. He did his best to act interested in what they were saying. Sometimes he was. Sometimes he wasn't. But they didn't need to know when he thought they were boring as hell, or, on some occasions, self-absorbed and arrogant little shits. Like the time he picked up a well-heeled middle-aged couple on Park Avenue. They were going to the opera at Lincoln Center. The husband was very friendly. Began talking with him right away. Asked him how his shift was going. His wife snapped at him. "Don't talk to the cabby, honey. He's just another servant." The husband caved, and that was that.

"I'd like to see Mount Everest. I don't want to climb it, but man, wouldn't it be great to see it in person."

"Anything else?"

"I'd like to be a Dad someday."

"Anything on the horizon?"

"Haven't met her yet." And then, thinking, why not, he said, "I've thought about doing some writing, short stories, I think. I have a hard time coming up with ideas. Complete ones. I can think of beginnings, but I have a hard time finding the endings."

"That stops you from writing?"

"Kind of."

"Rubbish. Don't let it. If I were you, I'd keep writing beginnings and if I couldn't find the ending, I'd just set it aside and start another beginning." She looked out the window at an elderly couple walking arm in arm. The woman was carrying a cup of what she decided was mint tea. "There's no avoiding endings anyway."

He was about to ask about her dreams when they pulled up in front of 330 West 30th Street. White letters on a blue awning announced the building as The French Apartments. The building's façade, crowned with a limestone balustrade adorned with four weather-worn flowered urn finials, bore an engraving: Société Française De Bienfaisance.

"It means French Benevolent Society," she said, anticipating his question. "Used to be the French Hospital run by nuns."

"Beautiful building. You lived here?"

"No. My mother was born here. She was adopted when she was a baby and never found her mother. From all I know, she really tried. Aunt Sally said my mother used to come here on her birthday almost every year, hoping her mother would show up."

"Sad."

"Brave."

For a few minutes, they sat silently. In nearly a whisper, she said, "Okay. Two more stops."

"Two more it is." He pulled away from the curb.

"I'd like to go by the Riviera down Seventh, you know it?"

"Riviera Café. Know it well, outside tables."

She nodded to him in the mirror. A cloud covered the sun, and the day darkened. When he turned south on Seventh Avenue, he slowed for a young couple crossing the street who were utterly oblivious to the approaching cab and three young men in their early twenties who saw it coming and didn't care; the cab could slow the hell down as far as they were concerned.

"I call them the invulnerables," she quipped.

"How's that?" he asked, giving the invulnerables time to pass and sparing their lives in the process.

"In their minds they're indestructible. Nothing can hurt them. I think we all go through a time when we think that. We hear about tragedies in the news, but it's like they happen to another kind of people. I don't know, like to some other species. It's the it-can't-happen-to-me syndrome. Then something sneaks up and pulverizes you and your it-can't-happen-to-me syndrome's gone forever."

A few minutes later they pull up in front of the Riviera Café on the corner of Seventh Avenue and Fourth Street. The café was comfortably situated in the sharpest angle of a block shaped like a triangle that, viewed from the air, would reveal itself to be a nearly perfect Isosceles triangle. Suggestion: The café was comfortably situated on a sharp-angled block that, viewed from the air, would reveal itself to be a nearly perfect Isosceles triangle.

"I love this place," she said. "I can't even count the number of times I've been here. Beautiful conversations. One of my best friends lives nearby, right around the corner. Wonderful staff." Then, after a pause: "The last time I was here I was proposed to."

"Did you accept?"

"God no. His name was Rick. I don't think I've ever loved anyone more than I loved him. But I knew when he was proposing he was involved with another woman."

"Jesus."

"Right. When you think about it though, people grow into their dysfunctions for real reasons."

"Doesn't mean they're not accountable."

"I ended the relationship less than two weeks after he proposed."

"Maybe it just means you haven't met Mr. Right yet."

"I know I won't find him," she said in a tone dark with sadness.

"Well...I hope you do," he said.

"Okay," she said, her voice energized. "Onto our last stop."

"And that is?"

"Two-twenty-eight West 15th Street." Her voice caught, fighting back tears.

Looking at her in the mirror. "Remember, you're a mystery, and that makes you special."

She smiled and nodded. "You're a sweet man, the world needs people like you."

Nearly fifteen minutes later and four minutes past three in the afternoon they arrived at 228 West 15th Street. A four story brick house with ground-level sliding glass doors.

She said, "Help me with my bags?" and handed him money for fare and tip.

"Sure. You moving here?"

"Yes."

"Looks nice, though moving's never easy."

"I'm hoping for nice."

"Me too."

He was approaching the entrance with a suitcase in each hand when he saw the brass plaque just to the left of the entrance. The two beautifully engraved words on the plaque registered just as the doors opened: Inwood Hospice.

He stopped walking. He suddenly felt dizzy and weak. He could feel her standing next to him. She gently took him by the elbow. "It's okay, I promise you. It's okay. I'm ready. You're welcome to visit me if you'd like."

"But isn't a hospice where people come to...?"

"Die. Yes."

"So how can I visit?"

She laughed. "I haven't scheduled it. I have time. I'm standing here with you, aren't I?"

He put down the suitcases and turned to face her. "May I please hug you?"

"Of course."

As they hugged, he said, "I'll visit you. Promise."

Later that evening, sitting at the kitchen table with a coffee and yellow pad, he picked up his pen and wrote, Once upon a time...

Checkout Love

He was in love with the cashier before he even got out of her checkout line, which means it happened fast because there was only one person in line in front of him. That person, an older man, and the bagger, an older woman, knew each other, were happy to see each other, and hugged each other. This compelled our soon to be smitten hero to say to the cashier, a beautiful woman with long white-gray hair cascading in waterfall ripples past her shoulders, "It's nice to see hugs like that."

"The world needs more hugs like that," she replied. She meant it. He could tell.

Before he could stop himself, he couldn't believe he heard himself say, "I hope you never dye your hair."

She smiled. "Not a chance."

And that was all it took. Full length smittification set in. He wasted not one of the twelve seconds it took him to leave the store. By the time he was halfway to the exit, he had proposed marriage. To his complete joy - and tectonic level of surprise - she accepted before he was out of the store.

As he left the store pushing his cart of groceries, the two of them were exiting the town hall where they'd just married. They'd agreed they would marry again, on a mountain, or a meadow, or by a lake, the ocean, settings they both cherished.

As he walked across the parking lot to his car, he realized their love-making that first night had taken them to a place of an amatory intimacy and depth neither had ever known before. The second night of lovemaking deepened their bond. After the second time she said: "What were you thinking about when we were doing it?"

"Willie Mays."

"You always think about baseball players when you're making love?"

"It keeps me going."

"Yeah. I couldn't figure out why you kept yelling, slide."

Just as he started the car, he realized they'd just repeated some of the exact bedroom-scene dialogue between Diane Keaton and Woody Allen in, "Play it Again, Sam."

By the time he pulled out of the store's parking lot for the three-and-a-half-mile drive home, they'd begun their life in an 1850 farmhouse nestled on the gentle slope of a lush green hill, just one mile outside a small village boasting a total of four shopkeepers and Mack & Ma's Eats, a coffee shop that served three meals a day, seven days a week. Late dinners were non-existent because M&Ms, as folks who knew it called it, closed promptly at 7 p.m., seven days a week.

His phone began buzzing, but he ignored it. They were in their first days together. Phone calls could wait. And, their early days were heaven, and Curran Highway was near empty both ways. They had conversations they hoped would never end; laughter so strong their stomachs hurt. They held hands and kissed each other gently, just because. The depth-of-heart in their lovemaking humbled them both. Their kissing was a love-filled language all its own.

All was going well for them until he took the left on Hodges Street, and then, moments later, as soon as he crossed over the Hoosic River, she began having second thoughts. By the time he made a right onto Church Street, she decided she needed space.

His phone started buzzing and again he ignored it. He was losing an angel, calls could wait. He was flabbergasted! What on earth had happened? He loved her his whole wide world! Wasn't that a good thing? Had he missed something, the poor sod?

But then too, he understood. Fear of loss, and then, more loss. Fear too of having your right to self, threatened. No matter its form, no relationship can be a healthy one if each person can't be who they are, safely and openly. It's the kind of principle most pledge allegiance to, and far less than most stand up for.

She moved out just as he pulled into the driveway of the two-story building where he lived, second floor, in a one-bedroom apartment. She'd left a note behind saying she'd contact him to let him know where to send her things.

The phone started buzzing again just as he turned off the engine. This time, he answered. It was the cashier from the market.

"Hi, I've been trying to reach you. You left your groceries in the parking lot." It seems he'd pushed the cart of groceries to his car, but he'd been distracted by the Woody Allen dialogue and never put groceries in his car.

"Oh man... I have the organizational skills of a tree stump."

She laughed. "Me too sometimes. Come on back now. We'll be waiting."

As he headed back, he wondered if they'd hug.

Bullets

When Harold puts the pistol in his mouth and pulls the trigger, he is sure, but the gun jams. Harold figures maybe he should rethink things. The birds were on the feeder that morning and the sun was up, so it wasn't like the trigger squeeze was weather related. He's just tired is all. Tired of getting up day after day and wading through twenty-four hours over and over again. A man can only take so much.

Harold is 48. He lives alone in the city. He hasn't always lived alone. Grew up in a family. Mother and father. Two brothers, two sisters, Harold in the middle, always in the middle. Even now Harold is in the middle. Like nearly everyone else he can think of, he is caught between the socially promoted vice grip of the urge to buy and the resulting need for more money. Even when you know the vice grip itself drives your greed and the greed of others, stopping is not only out of the question, but also a question rarely asked. The levels of greed in the community's bloodstream attenuates humanity.

For Harold, there is no family to speak of anymore. The whys of this truth don't matter. People die, people leave, people disappear. People become things other than people. As for friends, Harold has one or two, but not so many that his absence would make much of a difference. We're all going to die someday, aren't we, Harold would think, as he walked the streets near his home. So why can't I choose when? It's my fucking life.

Harold puts the pistol back in the dresser drawer and leaves the house. He walks down Wander Lane and turns right on Orchard Street. It's his favorite street, though he doesn't know why. He just feels at ease walking on Orchard, which, alas, runs for just two blocks. At the end of the two blocks Harold turns left and at the next corner reaches his destination. The Victory Diner.

Harold loves diners. Always has. There was something matter of fact about them. Something down to earth. Comforting. Sitting at the counter (Harold always sits at the counter) he orders bacon and eggs, home fries, coffee, and a large orange juice, which makes him laugh out loud because orange juice is healthy and when you're really fucking tired and close to the end, eating healthy is pretty much a moot point.

Emma the waitress is short and thick, a human square, with a mop of brown hair and a mustache. Harold doesn't understand how a woman can have a mustache and do nothing about it. But he never says anything. Emma treats him nice, always has. He likes her. So why wound?

"You look tired, Harold," Emma says, putting the coffee on the counter in front of him. Some spills over into the saucer.

"I am."

"You need sleep."

"That's about all I do."

"Then why you tired?"

Harold doesn't know the answer. He is saved from having to make one up when a large man with red hair waves Emma over. She waddles away to see what he wants.

One hour later Harold is back home staring at the pistol, wondering why it jammed. He cleans it regularly. It had been a gift from his friend Mort about eight years ago.

"You'll need this," Mort had said, handing him the black wood box that, when opened, revealed the .22 caliber pistol. "Never know what you'll run into, eh?"

"It's a twenty-two, Mort. Not much of a weapon."

"It is if you shoot somebody with it."

Mort had a point.

Harold took the gift because he didn't want to upset Mort who was just about as sweet and attentive a friend as one could ask for.

While he was kind and loyal, Mort didn't always have the best judgment. Once, when the annual marathon was being run through the city and everyone in the neighborhood was putting out tables filled with water, Gatorade, bananas, energy bars, Mort put out a table piled high with hefty peanut butter sandwiches on Wonder Bread. Looks of horror, confusion and astonishing levels of discomfort were seen on the faces of many runners who grabbed at the sandwiches hungrily only to have their jaws nearly welded shut by the large swaths of Skippy Mort had generously slathered on both pieces of bread before making them a sandwich.

Harold kept the pistol when Mort gave it to him, hoping he would never have to use it on anyone, including himself.

Now he is not so sure.

At home there is nothing for Harold except his books (he's read nearly all of them, some more than once) and his music (primarily jazz and classical) and, of course, his rock collection. He doesn't care what kind of rocks they are. That's not what's important to him. What's important to Harold is their look and feel. He prefers smooth surfaces. There is something about the strong cool surface he finds comforting, reassuring, soothing. The smoother, the better. The smoothness denotes an inexplicable refinement, thousands upon thousands of years of experience. The smoother the surface the more they can be counted on. They boast a kind of indestructibility. No matter what goes wrong, they'll still be there, something you can't say about nearly anything else. Not trees or houses or buildings, and sure as hell not people. But there are always rocks. And knowing there are always rocks calms him.

He'll pick up a rock and hold it tight in his hands. He keeps his eyes closed so he can better feel the cool of the surface. And then, when the surface of the rock warms to match his hands, he puts it down and picks up another. He does this over and over again. Each time the coolness soothes and relaxes him. Sometimes it helps him find his way to sleep, tears, laughter, answers, conclusions.

Harold is lonely.

He doesn't realize this yet, but he is. Loneliness is at the core of his being now, like a cancer, spreading, aching, endless, and, with it, comes a feeling of nonexistence.

Harold pays the check and leaves. He begins to walk. He always walks the streets of his neighborhood, never beyond. He wants home within reach. He rarely talks to anyone. He just walks. Sometimes he'll look in store windows at objects that interest him, usually things that shine with polished color. The glint of something shiny strikes him as a burst of life in and of itself. Reflections too, reflections are movement are they not? Movement can't occur when there is nothing. Movement is life. Harold keeps walking, keeps moving.

All night Harold walks. His legs ache, his feet grow damp from sweat and a rain that falls for half an hour just after midnight. He passes the all-night newsstand run by Georgie Bradshaw six times. Georgie says, "Hi, Harold," the first three times he passes, but gets no response. The next three times he just looks and shakes his head sadly. Georgie worries about Harold.

Katie Ann Buckles in the Victory Diner is worried too. Katie Ann takes over for Emma at six p.m. the time she starts her twelve-hour shift. This night Harold comes in twice asking for tea. Harold never drinks tea, so that's a concern right there. Both times Harold takes a few sips of his tea, gets up and leaves without paying. No one says a word the first time as Katie Ann pays for his tea. The next time the owner Sal Figueroa just waves his hand like he's brushing away cobwebs, nods his head and says, "Forget it. Boy's in pain, look at'm."

Harold keeps walking. He has some rocks in his pockets and their presence reassures him, though of what he has no idea. Harold grows afraid that if he stops walking the world would end. His world anyway, and if his world ends then what happens to the rest of the world is no concern of his. He realizes movement is the key to survival. If there's movement, you breathe. If there isn't, you don't.

He keeps walking.

It is just past three in the morning when Harold sees Father Jessup coming towards him. Father Philip Jessup is a large man with a brown beard and kind brown eyes. He'd grown up in the neighborhood and was once the starting linebacker for the Saint Ignatius varsity football team. All the girls back then wanted Philip Jessup, but Philip Jessup wanted to serve God, and so he did.

Seeing Harold, Father Jessup stops and smiles. "Harold, my boy. You're up late, or would I be wiser to say early?"

Standing now, Harold keeps walking in place, knowing if his movement stops, his world will end. "You're up awful late, Father."

"Tending to the flock, Harold. Old Mrs. Williams is fearing another stroke any minute, thinks it'll be her last."

"She's had a couple of'm hasn't she?"

"Good handful plus."

"How she doing now?"

"Fine, I'd say. We prayed, read some from the bible together, twenty-third psalm mostly. Some cups of tea. She's sleeping now."

"Can I ask you somethin' Father?"

"Of course, Harold. Of course." Father Jessup keeps his kind eyes fixed on Harold's, trying to pour as much love and kindness into the boy as he can.

"If a car runs out of gas, what then?"

"You get more gas."

"What if there ain't anymore?"

"Well then, I see your point. One could see that as a bit of a predicament one could."

"How can a car be worth anything if it doesn't have any gas?"

"Ah," Father Jessup says, his chin lifting as an understanding of something takes place behind his soft brown eyes. "There's often more than one kind of fuel, Harold. If there's no gas, I look for other fuel. It'd be a shame for (gently, now) someone to go to waste. Nothing comes about in God's world just to be wasted."

Harold nods thank you and stumbles along.

"You're always in my prayers, Harold," Father Jessup calls after him.

"Thank you, Father," Harold calls back without stopping or turning his head.

Harold keeps walking.

Just past four in the morning, Harold is talking out loud. He wants words filling the air around him. He doesn't care if anyone hears him. He is way past caring about things like that. He likes words, always has. When loosed, they are a source of life for him. When spun in the air, they are good company. They are proof he exists. When you are stuck inside loneliness remembering you exist can be one tough proposition.

Harold talks. "You tell me why I'm supposed to dream," he calls out, not sure where the words are coming from, and not much caring. They are what they are. "If I keep moving, I'm real right? Why should I be less real if I am still? Huh? Care to explain that?"

He is beginning to feel better. He sneezes and laughs out loud because it was a good sneeze and there is something enjoyable about a good sneeze.

"I liked that sneeze!" He laughs. "There are some good things in life, I know. I mean people are loved and that should be able to happen for me too."

Then, in a quiet voice: "So maybe, Harold, you should stick around. Yeah, yeah - I know. I'm damn fuckin' tired, though."

A few minutes before five a.m. Harold walks back into his apartment. He is exhausted. He takes of his shoes and jeans and makes himself a cup of coffee. He puts the coffee on the small table in the kitchen. He retrieves the pistol from the dresser drawer and places it on the table next to his coffee. Then he goes to his rock collection, chooses three of his favorite rocks, and brings them to the table. Before he sits down, he removes a slice of whole wheat bread from a loaf in the breadbox and eats it.

He sits down at the table, picks the gun up and slowly turns it in his hands, examining it very closely. He places it gently back on the table and takes a sip of coffee. He picks up one of the smooth rocks in his hand, closes his eyes, and holds it tight. He doesn't want to miss a moment of the rock's cool to warm journey. Once there, he places the rock down on the table, takes a sip of his coffee, and picks up the second rock. Again, he closes his eyes as the rock drifts from cool to warm. Tears now begin to spill from his eyes and drift down his cheeks. He picks up the third rock and again, cool to warm, the tears flow. There is movement when rocks go from cool to warm and where there is movement there is life. The world has plenty of rocks, each a source of movement, each a source of life.

He stands up, picks up the pistol, walks slowly into his bedroom, puts it to the side of his head, pauses, and puts it back in the dresser drawer. Not now, he thinks, shaking his head, figuring someday he might even buy bullets. But not now.

The Shirt

Maceo watches him rummaging through the battered wire wastebasket, thinking the tattered old man's looking for food or maybe a bottle of wine or beer with some left in it. People walk past him like he isn't even there. Couples push strollers with babies dressed in pastel colors, sunlight blazing, the day a welcome warmth in the mid-seventies. The tattered old man wears a filthy plaid sports coat, stained t-shirt, torn pants, worn shoes, no laces. Maceo looks over at his brother Roscoe leaning against a light post. Roscoe takes a hard drag off his Newport, watches the tattered old man, glances at Maceo. "Fucked up, man."

They'd come to Central Park for a free concert they both agreed sucked. The sound system kept going out. Couldn't find any girls either. Now, with the crowd breaking up and leaving, the brothers are focused on the tattered old man.

Maceo nods. "We should do something."

"Like what?"

The tattered old man yanks a newspaper from the basket, his brow furrows into a hard V, reads something intently, mutters, "Fuckin' Yankees," and shoves the paper back into the basket, giving it an extra shove, which doesn't get it deep enough to suit him, so he grabs a branch off the ground and jams the newspaper deeper into the basket, the hard V getting harder, stabbing at it. "Fuckin' Yankees."

Maceo smiles. "Maybe we can take him home."

Roscoe flicks his cigarette away. "You lost your fuckin mind? Take him home, and then what?"

"Feed him. Let him have a bath."

"We don't have enough hot water to clean'm."

"We can't just leave him."

"He was here when we got here. He's older'n we are. Made it this far."

"But we know about him now."

Roscoe lights another Newport. "I can't picture him on a bus."

"That'd be some sight."

Maceo and Roscoe live in a bungalow colony called Eleven Acres in Bardonia, a blip of a hamlet in Rockland County just north of New York City. Eleven Acres has half a dozen bungalows and one large white house carved up into five apartments. Maceo is 18, Roscoe, 17. While both know how to drive, they don't have a car. They take Red & Tan buses to the city.

Roscoe, thinking of the bus fare, says, "We have enough money?"

"Yeah."

Roscoe takes a slow drag from his Newport, glances up at the sky, looks at his brother still looking at the tattered old man who is now sitting on the ground next to the wire basket. He is rooting through his pockets, searching for a match to light the gnarled butt pulled from the trash now clamped in his mouth.

Maceo looks over at his brother who reads him and tosses him the lighter. Roscoe thinking, "He's gonna try'n rescue this fucking guy."

Maceo extends the lighter now, offers the tattered old man the safety of no eye contact by looking at the gnarled cigarette butt, let him experience something being given to him, "Need a light?"

The offer of a light lifts a pair of yellowed eyes to meet Maceo's. Maceo thinking the butt looks like the guy's fingers, bent and dirty. "Save the clip, man." Then, without turning away, "Roscoe, you got a smoke?" Roscoe offers the tattered old man a cigarette. The tattered old man hesitates before taking the cigarette lightly between thumb and forefinger, holding it out, arm extended, like it's red hot, his face clenched with suspicion. "What do you two want?"

"Nothing. You look like you could use a cigarette," Roscoe says.

"I figure you smoke it, it's one less cigarette to fuck him up," Maceo says, nodding at his brother.

"You brothers?"

They nod.

"Good. I like that. Looking out for your brother." The arm pulls in, the cigarette between forefinger and middle finger in a flash. "Still got that light?"

Maceo flicks the lighter on, the tattered old man draws hard, his cheeks pull so far in Roscoe wonders if they're touching in the middle of his mouth. As the cigarette tip glows to life, Maceo asks, "What's your name?"

The tattered old man doesn't answer, leans back, inhales, coughs a loud gagging cough. "Fuck! Menthol!"

"Newport," Roscoe says.

"Worse'n non-filters. Kill you in no time. Thank you though, fellas. Awfully nice of you." He takes another drag. This time he doesn't cough.

Maceo and Roscoe sit down on the grass next to the tattered old man whose head suddenly pops up as if he just got an idea. "Marvin."

The brothers look at him.

"My name's Marvin. Marvin Nathan Murphy."

Roscoe smiles. "Good name."

"Like hell it is," Marvin Nathan Murphy says, voice softening. "Think of the initials. M N M. Grew up getting called, M'n'm. Not fun, but funny, I grant you."

Maceo asks, "Where you live?"

"Where you sitting?"

"With you."

"You've found your answer."

Roscoe lights up a cigarette. "No family?"

"None to speak of. Have a daughter out there somewhere," Marvin Nathan Murphy looks around him as if his daughter might appear from out of nowhere. "Near 32 now. She's a mess like her Mom. Her Mom killed her heart a long time ago. Blamed the world on her, and what she couldn't blame on her, she blamed me. If there's an earthquake in Chile her Mom'd find a way to blame one of us, both of us if she could. Poor kid lived under the influence of that crazy bitch. Nothin' I could do. Every time she tried to get close to me her mother made her life living hell." Marvin Nathan Murphy grows a hard V and stares down at his cigarette as if an answer lurked somewhere in the shifting spiral of smoke. "She's a good kid down deep. Doesn't know it is all. Likely never will."

"She knows you're out here?"

"I don't think she'd much care."

Roscoe says, "But she's your daughter, man."

Marvin Nathan Murphy takes a drag off his Newport and looks at Roscoe. His eyes soften. "One of the biggest myths on planet earth is family loves you just because you're family. Can't think of another myth that's caused more carnage than that one."

Roscoe wags his head. "But she's family."

"Believing that myth my young friend is risky business. People suffer more pain and damage from believing family always loves you than from maybe anywhere else. Some people love you, some don't. Family has nothing to do with it. Faster you learn that the better off you are."

Roscoe, shaking his head, "That's harsh."

"I know it. That's life."

Maceo says, "Where you sleeping tonight?"

Marvin Nathan Murphy looks around. "Somewhere around here I expect. Shelters are high risk."

Roscoe thinking, Here it comes. Maceo says, "Why don't you come home with us?"

Marvin Nathan Murphy forms another hard V, stares first at the ground, then up, at the boys. To Roscoe he says, "What about you?"

Roscoe thinking, this guy sees right through me, looks over at his brother. Marvin Nathan Murphy says, "Don't look at him. Talk to me."

"I think you should come home with us," Roscoe says quietly.

Marvin Nathan Murphy smiles at him. "But you're not so sure though, are you?"

Roscoe thinks for a moment, grinds his toe in the dirt. Nodding towards Maceo he says, "He's always trying to save the world."

"And you know that's a tall order?"

"It's impossible."

"You're right. It is. Should he stop then?"

Roscoe laughs out loud. "Be a fish out of water if he did." Maceo, watching, feels so much love for his brother he wants to hug him right then and there.

Marvin Nathan Murphy turns his gaze to Maceo. "You're a fine lad and I for one hope you don't stop trying to save the world. But maybe this piece of the world is better off here."

Maceo smiles. "Where'd you learn to talk like that?"

"Like what?"

"You're a fine lad. I for one. This piece of the world."

"The king's English? You've got a good ear, son. I was a teacher in an earlier life."

Roscoe says, "No shit?"

Marvin Nathan Murphy smiles now, says, "No shit. An English teacher. Did you know the "King's English" was a fine book written by two brothers just like yourselves?"

The brothers shake their heads no.

"Yes sir. The Fowler brothers. Henry Watson Fowler and Francis George Fowler. Published the book in 1906."

Roscoe wags his head, distorting the lift of his cigarette smoke. "No way you should be out here."

"Because I know about the Fowler brothers?"

Maceo leans in towards Marvin Nathan Murphy. "No. Because no one should have to be out here. You can come home with us."

Marvin Nathan Murphy nods. "I could use a drink, you know. Helps me decide the harder matters."

Maceo, still leaning in, says, "That won't solve anything. Anyway, it's not a hard matter figuring out no one should be homeless."

"Touché, young man. Touché." Looking up at the sky,

Marvin Nathan Murphy thinks for a minute, looks at the boys, slaps the palms of his hands on his knees, and nods. "Okay then."

Marvin Nathan Murphy nearly changes his mind when he learns the brothers live outside the city. Like many city dwellers, homeless or not, outside the city is not just another country, it's another world. Even worse, Marvin Nathan Murphy learns getting to the brothers' home means going on a bus ride, a bus ride long enough to stir up anyone's penchant for motion sickness. Marvin Nathan Murphy knows the universe has laws. He knows the ocean's tides and currents adhere to these laws. The Earth orbits the sun, the moon orbits the Earth. The universe has laws. Marvin Nathan Murphy knows about another law of the universe. Boys with red hair vomit on buses. Every time Marvin Nathan Murphy has been on a bus traveling any further than, say, a few blocks, a red-headed boy is on the bus and before the ride is over, the red-headed boy vomits. He had to. The universe has laws. Marvin Nathan Murphy has hated buses since he was a boy.

Maceo on the bus now heading north, sitting next to his brother wishes the bus wasn't so crowded. Wishes he and Roscoe had a fucking car because an elderly lady with a feather in her hat is having a rough time sitting next to Marvin Nathan Murphy who, in addition to smelling like a piece of sunbaked street meat, has been dry heaving for the last ten minutes.

The brothers are sitting next to each other and Marvin Nathan Murphy is three rows behind them, sitting on the aisle.

Roscoe leans over. "This ain't going too good, Mace."

Still looking out the window, Maceo says, "We're almost there," knowing damn well they weren't.

Roscoe shakes his head. "Hope he doesn't die on us."

A loud, "Argh!" from Marvin Nathan Murphy fills the bus.

Maceo chuckles. "He's not a happy man."

For reasons his young mind didn't fully understand, Roscoe always thought of Maceo as a kind of mountain. Not in the physically big sense. Maceo was built lean and strong and stood five-foot seven-inches tall, making him three inches shorter than Roscoe. No, it isn't Maceo's physical size that makes Roscoe think, Mountain. It's his larger-than-life presence. With dark brown eyes set strong under dark eyebrows, Maceo is remarkably prescient, quick to smile and laugh, attentive to everything in the moment he's in, and fiercely protective. Although Roscoe himself is powerfully built and fully capable of holding his own in a fight (he crushed Johnny McKinney's nose with a streak of a jab after all) Maceo has always been his protector. More than once, Roscoe has asked him to maybe back the fuck off a little and let him fight his own fight. Maceo would just give him a look and say, "When I'm not here, you fight. In the meantime, relax."

Once, when he was 15, Roscoe found himself cornered by three bullies in the batting cage at the Elmo Park baseball field on Cedar Drive. The three boys were not only bigger than Roscoe, but they were also older. One was 18, two were 19. They wanted Roscoe's glove. Although he was physically no match for the bullies, Roscoe was not hurting for courage. So even though he was scared out his ever-loving mind, he had no intention of backing down. The three bullies were closing in on him when all four were brought up short by a rage-filled scream that came from behind them. "Time to die!"

It was Maceo. He was riding his bike across the rutted field and with a baseball bat raised over his head screaming, "Die motherfuckers!" at the top of his lungs over and over again.

The three bullies were dumbstruck at the sight of this wild-haired wild-eyed 16-year-old boy with a baseball bat and full head of steam coming right at them. They didn't move, at least not right away. When Maceo got within ten yards of them, they saw murder in his eyes and fled.

Walking off the field together, Roscoe pushing Maceo's bike, Roscoe said, "Think you could've taken'm?"

Maceo laughed. "Fuck no. They would've killed me. Crazy scares people is all. Remember that."

Roscoe watches his brother whisper, "How you doin'?" in response to a group of school kids waving at the passing bus. Roscoe smiles, leans over and gently touches his brother's shoulder with his head. Not breaking his gaze out the window, Maceo smiles. Leaning their head against each other has been a form of affection between the brothers since their father died suddenly when Maceo was 15 and Roscoe was 14. He'd taken ill with an intestinal blockage that led to peritonitis. Killed him in three days. Both boys were shattered. Their father was their hero. The greatest gift life ever gave them. Both held tight to his memory as if their lives depended on it. Particularly since their mother, never fond of being a mother, threw Maceo out of the house when he turned 18 with Roscoe following in his footsteps one year later.

As the bus pulls into their stop, Roscoe and Maceo are up and heading down the aisle, relieved to have the bus ride behind them. Marvin Nathan Murphy struggles to his feet and, once standing, turns his attention to the elderly lady with the feather in her hat who is gazing fixedly out the window. "A thousand pardons, madam. You were gracious throughout this most difficult ride."

Without turning her head, the elderly lady with a feather in her hat says. "Take a bath and brush your teeth for God sakes."

Marvin Nathan Murphy pauses, turns to leave, pauses again, and turns back. "My body and teeth can be cleaned madam, but sad though it may be, the same can't be said for your character." And with that, Marvin Nathan Murphy makes his way down the aisle towards the exit.

Just as Marvin Nathan Murphy is about to get off the bus, he hears a young boy say, "Feel better, mister." He looks over his shoulder in the direction of the voice and sees a boy of about 10 smiling at him. The boy has red hair. So much for the laws of the universe, Marvin Nathan Murphy thinks, as he nods a thank you to the boy and hurries off the bus.

Marvin Nathan Murphy stops walking when he sees the brothers' bungalow, a weathered rundown affair with a scuffed up black front door. The place looks small. The boys, they were boys after all, seemed proud of their digs. Maceo opens the front door with his key then stands aside for
Marvin Nathan Murphy and his brother.

The front door opens into a surprisingly large kitchen with a nice-size dining area. The floor is linoleum sporting a faded floral design on a muddy-white background. The walls are painted a yellow so bright Marvin Nathan Murphy finds himself contemplating the need for sunglasses. A round table against the far wall is surrounded by four chairs that don't match. The refrigerator, sink, stove, and counter run along the opposite wall. There is a window over the sink and another window in the wall on the far side of the room. There are no curtains.

There is a small four-by-four foot hallway off the kitchen with doors to three rooms: a small bathroom provided a home to toilet, small sink, shower stall. Roscoe's room is to the left and Maceo's to the right. There is no living room.

Putting on coffee now, Maceo listens to Marvin Nathan Murphy. "Fine home, my boys. A fine home indeed. Any hair of the dog about?"

"Thanks, Mr. Murphy." Roscoe says.

Maceo now. "Not at the moment. Wanna shower?"

To the boys' surprise, Marvin Nathan Murphy blushes. Quietly, as if carefully placing the word in the air before him for closer examination, he says, "Shower."

The boys stand quiet, not moving, instinctively knowing they are in a tender fragile moment for Marvin Nathan Murphy, knowing it is best to let him move through it at his own pace.

A few minutes later, Maceo gently places a mug of black coffee on the table in front of Marvin Nathan Murphy with a nod for him to sit down if he'd like. Marvin Nathan Murphy lowers himself so slowly into the chair you'd think he fears it will shatter if he sits at normal speed. He reaches out and briefly touches the rim of the coffee mug. He bows his head and stares at the floor between his feet. By now his stench has filled the room, which is not why tears flood the eyes of both boys.

"We got extra towels," Roscoe says.

Not looking up, Marvin Nathan Murphy nods. "Don't see the point in it though."

"In what?" Roscoe asks.

"A shower. These are the only clothes I have. I shower, then what? Get back into these filthy things?"

Maceo and Roscoe exchange looks. Maceo says, "We got clothes for you."

Tears begin to spill from Marvin Nathan Murphy's eyes cutting pale paths down his face, one falls onto the back of his hand, a tiny pool of heartbreak.

"Mr. Murphy," Roscoe begins before Marvin Nathan Murphy gently cuts him off saying, "Jesus, kid. If you're gonna offer me clean clothes and a shower not to mention this fine cup of coffee, least you can do is call me Marvin."

Roscoe smiles. "Okay, Marvin. We got clothes for you, please don't worry about it."

Marvin Nathan Murphy in the shower now luxuriates in the hot water falling on his worn body. He scrubs himself with a washcloth and a bar of soap producing all kinds of welcome foam. He's already shampooed his hair three times having squeezed out huge dollops from the large bottle of Herbal Essence shampoo he found in the shower rack. Marvin Nathan Murphy, smiling now, thinking the feel of hot water and soap on the human body had to be pretty damned close to what heaven is like.

In Maceo's room the brothers are going through the closet.

Roscoe finds a pair of dark blue sweatpants for Marvin Nathan Murphy, locates a pair of socks, underwear, and a clean undershirt. Suddenly, the boys' face a tough decision.

The only long sleeve shirts they have are flannel shirts that belonged to their father. Both boys liked to press their face into the shirts and breathe in. Even though their father has been dead for four years, love-driven memories bring his scent back to them from deep within the soft flannel folds.

"Fuck," Roscoe says quietly, shaking his head. "What do we do?"

"We know the answer. We let him borrow a shirt so he can be warm. We'll get him some shirts at Sears tomorrow. For tonight he can wear one of these."

"Dad would want him to be warm," Roscoe says.

"That's the one," Maceo says, reaching in and gently removed a navy blue, white-and-gray-checked flannel shirt from the hanger.

Roscoe nodding, says, "Perfect."

Marvin Nathan Murphy drying himself now with the towels the boys gave him, smells each of his armpits. Nothing! He smiles and continues drying himself. He is pretty much all dry now but doesn't want the feel of the soft towels against his skin to stop, not ever.

A soft knock on the bathroom door and one of the boys, he can't tell which, reaches in and hands Marvin Nathan Murphy clean clothes. "Thanks, boys. Thanks ever so much."

The feeling doesn't last. Sitting on the toilet now, clothes in his lap, head bowed, Marvin Nathan Murphy feels it hit. The all too familiar palm drenching fear, every wrinkle in his tired face a rivulet carved in his soul, hands trembling, legs too. He thinks about taking another shower, hesitates, what will the boys think? The shower on, off, then on again. He bends forward now, stomach knotting up, folding him up, sweaty. Marvin Nathan Murphy thinking, I am all alone. There is no one anymore. The words, all alone, a death sentence passed, and executed. The death of the life he was supposed to have, now so far away it's little more than a barely remembered landscape, leaves him with no life at all. Who on earth does he think he is to even contemplate a new beginning, starting over? He remembers her. Her exquisite laugh, her shape, the dancing magnificence of her mind. There he was, 25 years old, Cristina, 23. Their love and their love making took them to a place neither'd believed possible. Then, slave to his history, came his violence, his infidelities. He destroyed their relationship and nearly destroyed her, the very person he loved most in the world. She was still that person. When she left him that cold February night, he felt the light that was Marvin Nathan Murphy go out.

"I am all alone," he whispers, the terror now a vice grip. Save for his breathing, he believes himself dead.

From the kitchen the boys hear the shower turn on again. Roscoe looks at Maceo who is at the stove cooking up burgers and franks. "Another shower?"

"Good for him."

"Gotta be hell living like that. What do we do about his drinking?"

"I don't know, bro. Maybe he sees he's got a place here, some clean clothes. Maybe he puts the bottle down. First thing is, feed him."

"He's a nice guy."

"That he is."

The kitchen table is a wasteland of crumbs, drops of mustard and ketchup, relish, crumpled napkins, slivers of onion. The hamburgers and hotdogs have been eaten. Maceo and

Roscoe each downed two dogs and two burgers. Marvin Nathan Murphy had one each. All are full, all are smiling, and now all are having coffee - what the boys' father used to call the pot of gold at the end of any respectable culinary rainbow.

Outside, after dinner, Roscoe, and Marvin Nathan Murphy fire up Newports. Maceo nurses a fresh mug of coffee, looks over at Marvin Nathan Murphy. Freshly shaved, hair washed and combed, he recognizes a remarkable depth and kindness in the older man's face. He looks comfortable in clean clothes, in his father's flannel shirt.

The two brothers decided earlier not to tell him it was their father's shirt. While they liked Marvin Nathan Murphy, telling him would be handing over too much of themselves.

Watching Marvin Nathan Murphy smoke his cigarette Roscoe thinks maybe Maceo was right to bring him home. Finding him part-time work shouldn't be all that hard.

"What's tomorrow bring, boys?"

"Tomorrow's Sunday," Maceo says. "We thought maybe we'd cook up a big breakfast then take you around, let you see the sights. Give you an idea of where you are."

Marvin Nathan Murphy looks up at the darkening sky. "Sounds like solid plan to me."

"Cool," Roscoe says.

"You are two fine young men."

"Thank you, Marvin," Maceo says.

"Yeah, thanks Marvin," Roscoe says.

"Time for me to get some shut eye. Been awhile since I've been in a real bed. You guys got any writing paper?"

Maceo's says, "Sure. You write?"

Marvin Nathan Murphy emits a soft laugh. "Old habits die hard, my boy. Like to scribble things from time to time."

Roscoe says, "Be right back." Moments later he hands Marvin Nathan Murphy a pad and pen.

"Thank you, boys," Marvin Nathan Murphy says, "Night now."

"Night, Marvin."

It is just past five thirty in the morning when Roscoe finds the note. He reads it, then quickly goes in, and shakes Maceo awake. "He's gone."

"What?" Maceo says, coming out of sleep.

"Marvin's gone."

Maceo sits straight up, mutters, "Shit," and gets out of bed. "Maybe he just went out for a bit."

"He left a note, Mace. He's gone, he's not coming back."

"Where's -?"

"On the kitchen table."

Maceo sitting at the table now reads the note out loud.

Roscoe sits across the table from his brother and listens.

Dear Boys

Thank you both for your kindness, generosity, for the food and the clean clothes. Most of all, thank you for your friendship. Too much time has passed for me to be able to change who I am in my journey. I'm sorry I'm leaving without saying goodbye in person. I'm ashamed to admit it, but I can't handle face-to-face goodbyes anymore. Strange how life can let me have the gift of meeting two young men to love and admire while denying me the strength to stay here and live out your offer of a what some might call a second chance, a new beginning. No matter. I will carry the two of you in my heart forever. Take care of each other. I know you will. Thank you for helping an old man discover he can still have meaning to others.

Marvin

Neither boy says a word. Soon they are standing in the front of the bungalow looking across the field. The front door of the bungalow is open and the scent of coffee cooking in the coffee maker drifts into the cool morning air.

Finally, Roscoe says, "You tried, Mace."

"You did too."

In a quiet, tender voice, Maceo says, "He's got Daddy's shirt."

"That's good. Daddy'd be glad."

"Yeah, I think so too."

Roscoe nods, then gently touches his brother's shoulder with his head.

The Opening

A spring rain slowly put out the fire, one force calming another in the early, overcast morning. Slinky wisps of black smoke curled out from beneath the car's blackened hood. The dog's teeth sank into the charred thigh and tore off a bite. Had anyone been in the rubble-filled lot within arm's length of the dog, they would have seen half its right ear was missing. From a greater distance, the dog was nothing more than a spectral silhouette, a shapeshifter in the morning mist. The dog freed another bite.

A few yards away, shriveled junkies slow shuffled in and out of a jagged black hole in an abandoned building bordering the west side of the lot. Inside, they fed their hunger. They had no idea an old homeless man had crawled into what he mistakenly believed was the safety of an abandoned car, only to die in his sleep a short time later when his heart attacked, his body convulsed, and his heart stopped. Less than an hour later, two of the shriveled doused the vehicle with gasoline, and set it on fire for warmth, and fun. They never saw the dead body crumpled on the floor behind the front seats. The dog snarled off a curious rat, tore off another bite, and vanished into the ragged black hole.

It was ten past six in the morning. Had you seen the belching primordial lot just then, you might have thought the end of the world was nigh.

Shuckle Jones had seen. The sixty-two-year-old had been sitting at his second-floor kitchen window overlooking the lot with the day's first coffee. He saw the dog disappear into the black hole. With partially detached curiosity he watched two junkies wilt into shifting, angular piles on the ground. Moments later, their ambulatory skills returned, they too vanished into the black hole to feed their hunger.

The rain picked up again. Like every being on the planet except the dog, Shuckle had no idea there was a dead man in the car. Had he known, he would have understood. Staying alive sometimes boiled down to survival of the luckiest.

He was glad the dog had found shelter. The dog, called Brown Dirt Dog by everyone in the neighborhood, was a friend. He was always catching the dog peering in at him through the kitchen window from the fire escape. A pile of rubble that leaned against a partially collapsed wall allowed the dog climb up to the fire escape, sit just outside Shuckle's kitchen window, and look inside. It was clear the dog wanted to move in and make himself at home. As much as he'd grown to love the dog and knew damn well the company would do him good, his instinct was to protect his sanctuary of quiet, and stillness. He kept the screen lowered and security gate locked.

Shuckle Jones poured a second cup of black coffee out of the dented metal percolator he'd rescued from a garbage pail on East Third Street two years ago. He sat down again, brushed a mass of wavy gray hair off his forehead, and looked out the window. The police and fire department had arrived. Splashes of red and blue light danced on the kitchen walls and ceiling. Shuckle watched them wet down the car and remove what was left of the charred body. Shuckle muttered, damn, and wondered, only for a moment, who the dead man was. He brushed the question away.

At his age, Shuckle had his fair share of aches and pains, but things could be worse. He walked two hours every day, no matter the weather. He played handball and racquetball, solo for the most part. He liked the jazz-like body movement he experienced when he played. All of you in the moment, the place you were most meant to be, he believed.

He'd disengaged from anything really competitive years ago. Wasted energy. He did, however, play handball with Willie Turnbuckle. Willie was a retired city mechanic who lived two floors up in 4C. Games with Willie were background music to their conversations, which liked to roll on unabated, save for those infrequent moments when a hotly contested sequence of play required a focus only made possible by the absence of speech. Grunts, snarls, single nostril blowing, throat clearings, and wordless shouts, were all considered fair play. These were the sounds that came with the territory.

Shuckle and Willie figured they split their games roughly fifty-fifty. It was nothing more than a guess. They never kept score.

"Aging is not for the squeamish," Shuckle once quipped between games. "Why do we put up with it?"

Willie Turnbuckle laughed. "We have a choice?"

Shuckle finished his coffee, rinsed his mug out in the sink, put it in the dish rack, went into the living room, and sat down at the round oak table in the corner by the window. He picked up one of the twenty something pencils he'd sharpened earlier that morning, opened his composition book, and began writing.

Early in the wake of his sixtieth birthday he'd realized - finally - that getting published had damned little to do with how well you wrote and a whole lot to do with who you knew. Shuckle really didn't care anymore who read his work, or if it got published. He wrote, that's what he did. Sometimes, because he liked to, and always, because he had to. As rain pelted the living room window, Shuckle Jones wrote about the one person he did want to read his work.

The first time we made love was the first time I'd ever made love in my life. She'd undressed to her panties. She was shy. In bed she faced away from me, her delicately sculpted back, pristine. I remember her shoulders, the cut of her shoulder blades, the sweet, delicious curve of her hips, her hair glistening wheat gold. And she was nervous too! I'm not sure why. She was the angel.

I remember I was trembling. I touched her shoulder gently, and she turned to face me. I pulled the blanket back to see all of her. She was exquisite, slender, her small breasts, pure perfection. I wondered who the first fool was to arrive at the absurd idea that thin was not shapely. You don't always need an amplifier to hear the music.

We were in each other's arms discovering, then and there, that two can become one. Beyond the reach of doubt, I realized that my earlier understanding of making love was frayed, fragmented, false, misguided, disfigured, completely wrong. I was so filled with her presence, how close she was, I thought I'd burst into a thousand stars from the joy. Her scent dizzied me. I could feel and taste her, all without   moving. It was as if I was filled with sunlight and its source was in my arms, and I was in her arms, and, for reasons I could not begin to fathom, she loved me back.

Intimacy with Cristina was a beautiful world unto itself. While my understanding of love at the time, what it was to love, to be loved, possessed some accuracy, it would take me years to realize understanding something and living something were two distinct realities that can be worlds apart. When healthy, ours had been a ubiquitous intimacy, complete, without borders. It pulsed with life. It was an intimacy we'd both dreamed of, hoped for, and, I believe, deserved. It was an intimacy, it shreds me to say, I would prove staggeringly unready for and ultimately destroy.

Shuckle Jones put his pencil down, looked at his hand; he could see his age. The hand still looked strong, but his age, he could see it, and it scared him. He believed his worth lived in his words, living beings all, pulses eternal. Any difference he'd make - maybe - in the lives of others, or even one other, would come from his words. It was not lost on him (it never had been) that it was Cristina who'd helped him more than anyone else to grow his understanding of writing. That writing could mean joining the moment you were in or leaving it.

When the sun came out later that morning, Brown Dirt Dog and Shuckle took a walk down Houston Street. Shuckle liked watching the dog read the world with his nose, sniffing everything noticeable to him only, fully absorbed in that small, intimate space between nose and object of import: sidewalk, tree, old shoe, that experience-packed space, right there in the middle. As Shuckle walked, he relaxed. Movement connected him to life. The sun warmed him. Surrounded by old buildings, empty lots, the sounds of the street, the anxious sounds of cars, the perpetual movement of hurried pedestrians, some loudly prattling back and forth with each other, while others hurried on alone. When Shuckle and the dog walked past Katz's, a honey-gold movement from inside stirred a memory Shuckle's conscious mind left untouched.

Minutes later, sitting on a bench, Brown Dirt Dog curled up at his feet, Shuckle leaned back, sighed, smiled, and looked around. He saw backpacks on young sinewy shoulders, foolish young minds dragging on cigarettes, a curled-up elderly man, or woman, he couldn't tell, was tucked into one corner of a park bench, face covered with a blanket. He caught the sweet scent of pot that blossomed out from behind someone's cupped hands. He felt fully alive. He was part of something. He belonged to the world, however tenuous the tie.

Shuckle's conscious retrieved the memory of a honey-gold, ineffably familiar movement in Katz's window. He stood up and started back to Katz's with the dog.

There was no honey-gold in Katz's window now. Even so, he felt the presence of something unfinished. The breeze increased a notch or two and became wind. He looked at the dog. "The hawk's kicking, brother. A cup of tea would do me good. Wait for me." He knew this was a request Brown Dirt Dog felt no obligation to heed. The thought of walking home without the dog saddened him.

Ollie was behind the counter. He was sixty-two. The childhood friends found comfort in their common age. Ollie was tall and slender with twinkly brown eyes sheltered under a cornice of shaggy gray eyebrows, with a shaggy gray beard to match. A white apron was forever looped over his lanky frame.

"How are you this morning, Mr. Jones?"

"Morning, Ollie."

"Tea?"

"Please. I'm with my friend."

"Ah, the dog."

"Never argues."

"Bless him." Ollie poured the tea. "Saw you pass by earlier."

Shuckle nodded and watched the plume of steam rise and disappear.

"Thought you might've seen her."

"Could I get a corned beef on rye with that, Ollie?"

Ollie placed the glass of tea on the counter. "You hear what I said there, Mr. Jones?"

"Sorry, bro. No."

Ollie decided he'd make the sandwich and let his friend sit down and eat before he told him.

"Some pickles'd do me."

"Sit, I'll bring it to you. Anything else?"

Ollie brought Shuckle Jones his food and joined him at their favorite table by the window. What he had to say made him long for a talent in delicate delivery. He didn't want to bruise with anything resembling bluntness. Shuckle hadn't seen her in something like forty years. For Ollie, it had been something like thirty. Not long after she'd moved to Paris some twenty-odd years earlier, she married a man from Denmark who believed he was the reincarnation of Matisse. When Ollie looked up and saw her smiling at him across the counter that morning, he thought he was dreaming.

"Ollie." Her voice was familial.

"Cristina?" He'd of course known it was Cristina. The question was a poor attempt to shed the moment's dreamlike quality.

"How are you, Ollie?" She leaned closer. "I'm so sorry about Jane. I couldn't believe it."

Last winter Ollie's wife Jane was knocked out cold when she slipped and fell on a patch of ice. The nitwits at the hospital sent her home with instructions to take aspirin, rest, and use an icepack for the lump on her head. Ollie woke up the next morning to discover his wife of twenty-nine years, dead. The hospital had missed the brain bleed. Her brown eyes were open, vacant, dry. He lay there next to her for nearly an hour. There were so many things he still needed to tell her, wanted to tell her, to ask her, but they'd run out of time. When they took her away, it would be forever. He didn't want to rush forever.

He and Cristina clasped hands across the counter. "Thank you, Cristina." Ollie came out from behind the counter and broke tradition. He took off his apron and draped it over the back of a chair before they hugged hello.

"You didn't have to do that, Ollie," she said, nodding at the apron. "I love French food, but I miss New York and New York food. Wearing some is fine by me; it's still home."

"Are you staying?"

"We'll talk." She wrote her number on a piece of paper and gave it to him. She was staying with her friend Marlys in the West Village. "I have to go in a little bit. Marlys is out of town, and I promised to walk her dog. Call me, we'll catch up. Lunch tomorrow?" He nodded. Ollie was convinced, as much as he was convinced of anything these days, she had no intention of mentioning Shuckle, which is exactly why he went a little loopy for a moment when she said, "How's Shuckle?"

Ollie said the only words he could locate. "He's good. We can talk tomorrow if you'd like."

"I would."

Looking at Shuckle Jones now, it occurred to Ollie that sixty-two years of life had taught him there were certain things that needed to be said in a straight line. "I saw Cristina today." Shuckle Jones looked out the window and held still. He tried to lose himself in the movements of the pedestrians, the cars, the teenage girl on just the other side of the window who was trying valiantly to untangle her white toy poodle from the blue, sequined leash looped around one of the dog's back legs. He'd heard his friend. Losing Cristina was one of his deepest wounds, made all the more pulverizing so because it was self-inflicted. It had been his temper, his violence, verbal and physical. She'd tried. No one could've tried harder to make a marriage work than she did, and no one, he knew then and now, ever loved him more. Ending the marriage was unquestionably the healthiest choice. She deserved to be safe, and he required the emotional pulverizing that came with losing her in order to go into treatment and be fully committed to staying in treatment until he got well.

It took him time to fully digest the reality that the person who sobbed uncontrollably after a burst of violence, swearing he'll never do it again, was just like the alcoholic-addict clinging to the porcelain throne, swearing he'll never use again. They mean it when they say it, but without a real unflinching commitment to get well, the danger would live on.

So, Shuckle went into treatment with massive amounts of commitment. In his heart of hearts, he never wanted to hurt anyone. Anger was emotion. Verbal violence and physical violence were behaviors. Violence rarely deserved a pulse. Killing the pulse would take time. Shuckle took the time and killed the pulse. Turning to his friend, Shuckle said the only thing he could put into speech. "How is she?" He did not see Brown Dirt Dog uncurl to standing and walk away.

"She was Cristina."

Shuckle realized he was trembling. He felt cold. He slid his hands under his thighs to warm them.

"She asked how you were."

Shuckle reeled at the unexpected and unsettling appearance of hope, a distrusted feeling if ever there was one, that needed only a frail thread of reason to lead him back into its shaky arms. "What did you tell her?"

"Nothing really. We're grabbing a bite to eat tomorrow."

"I have to go home, Ollie."

Ollie nodded. "I know."

The following morning Shuckle Jones woke up exhausted from a nightmare. In it, he was required to witness the deaths of four people, two he knew, two he didn't. The deaths themselves would take place two at a time in two separate locations in barren rooms. All would die by lethal injection.

Standing in pale white room, he watched as the poison entered the first two. Their still-breathing bodies heaved and jerked and trembled before stillness arrived. Their faces looked mottled, puffy. The scene changed, and he found himself in the lobby of his apartment building. At one end of the lobby, two men sat behind a gray metal desk. One looked to be in his eighties, the other, somewhere in his forties. Shuckle recognized the younger man but couldn't remember his name. Shuckle approached. "Where are they?" They told him it was one-fifteen in the afternoon and the two he cared about had gone to St. Vincent's Hospital to die. This confused Shuckle because St. Vincent's had closed years ago. The younger man said, yes, that was true, but a corporation recently bought the building and a room had been made available for the two who needed to die. They didn't know the corporation's name, and anyway, did it really matter?

Shuckle charged up the stairway to his room where he knew he had enough money for cab fare to the hospital. He sobbed, stumbled. His nose was runny. He found two old ladies with very long hair, wearing flannel pajamas, sitting in his room. One was sitting on his bed, the other in his reading chair. When they saw him, they covered their mouths with kerchiefed hands and giggled. They told him it was still his room, and they hoped he was having a good day. Then, as if answering the call of some inaudible signal, they scuttled out of the room. He pulled a handful of soaking wet bills from under his mattress and shoved them into his front pants' pocket. He raced downstairs into the street his right arm waving. A cab swerved and skidded to a stop. In the cab he fell asleep, and, with a jolt, woke up in his bed, sweating, crying, and wondering what the fuck the dream was really about.

In the kitchen, he started a fresh pot of coffee and sat in a reading chair across from his bed to wait. His bed was a mattress on the floor surrounded by stacks of books. He was a man of certain habits and one of them was preparing the coffee machine the night before, so in the morning the only thing standing between him, and the day's first coffee was the push of a button.

Recently, and not for the first time, Shuckle found himself having to resist the notion of letting Brown Dirt Dog live with him. He remembered Steinbeck once wrote something to the effect of, we're creatures of habit, a very senseless species. Shuckle figured he had a point. Living alone without another living being had become a comfortable habit. If something happened to Brown Dirt Dog now, if a car or another dog killed him, he'd be heartbroken. But, if the dog lived with him, the intimacy that would come with living together made the prospect of the dog dying appear utterly unendurable.

Shuckle knew Ollie and Cristina were meeting today. She couldn't possibly want to see him, much less want him back. He knew better than that. He knew the hell he'd put her through. He knew he was batshit back then. So no, she didn't want him back. Perhaps when she'd asked after him, she was hoping for bad news. He couldn't blame her in the least. He'd long ago given up figuring out a way to forgive himself for the pain he'd caused her.   Shuckle was at peace with his life these days. While it wasn't exactly overflowing with activity, he had his books, his writing, friendships, Ollie, coffee, and, yes, the dog, and, the sound of rain, and thunder.

Out in the hall, his neighbor from across the hall, Eleanor Diddle (an unfortunate surname if ever there was one), was yelling at her husband. "Victor, you no good drunk fuck sonuvabitch, you're killing me!"

Victor now. "You drank everything, not a drop for me, piece of shit!"

Shuckle Jones knew to stay out of it. In fact, they could just go ahead and kill each other as far as he was concerned, the extra quiet would be nice. Just days after the Diddles moved in, he'd made the mistake of suggesting they not scream at each other in the hallway. Eleanor immediately threw the remaining cream of mushroom soup she'd been holding in a large cup all over his 1994 New York Rangers Stanley Cup Champion sweatshirt, while Victor Diddle snapped, "M-Y-O-B! M-Y-O-B!" He felt the sudden urge to dribble husband and wife out of the building at the same time. He'd been too short for basketball, but he'd always been able to dazzle his friends with his dribbling skills.

Victor Diddle surprised him two days later when he approached him in the hallway and apologized. "Sorry 'bout the other day, Shuckle, is it?"

Shuckle nodded.

"If I hadn't yelled at you, she would have made me wear that soup." He looked away for a moment, considering. "I hate cream of mushroom."

Shuckle Jones poured himself another cup of coffee and returned to his reading chair. He saw his father sitting on the couch. "Coffee, Dad?"

"No. Thank you, Shuckle." He looked at his father. His father smiled at him. Shuckle thought his father probably had the most beautiful smile he'd ever seen.

"I never stopped loving her, Dad."

"I know."

Shuckle leaned back in his chair and closed his eyes. When he opened them again, the couch was empty. It was eleven in the morning and still no call from Ollie. Had he already met up with Cristina? Maybe Ollie was holding off calling him with bad news, or, even worse, was on his way over to give him the bad news in person! He went into the kitchen, pulled a chair over to the kitchen window, sat down, and looked outside. He felt hopeless. He watched Brown Dirt Dog rooting through some recently tossed garbage bags, his motions compact, intense, focused.

"The industrious dog."

Memories swarmed him. Cristina went home to Rio Piedras in San Juan in December 1977, nearly forty years ago now, to be with her family for Christmas and New Year's. She'd been born in Maracaibo, Venezuela to a father hailing from Vermont, and a mother from Texas. What were the odds? When she left for the holidays, her absence made Shuckle realize, accept, and truly digest the fact he was so completely off-the-ground in love with Cristina, remaining just friends was no longer in the cards for him. The question was, of course, was it in the cards for her, for this one extraordinary woman who, by simply being herself, allowed them both to discover that the universe truly was in a more perfect alignment when they were together. He wrote her a letter telling her he was beyond-words in love with her, and if she didn't feel the same, he would understand, but he would have to distance himself because if he didn't, he only half-joked, he'd wind up in a rubber room playing with different colored blocks. He'd mailed it so it would be waiting for her when she returned home. When she returned home and read it, she called him. When he answered the phone, the first words she said were, "I love you, too."

Ollie waited twenty minutes for Cristina at a table by the window. For a moment, he worried she'd changed her mind and decided not to come. It would be unlike the Cristina he knew not to call and tell him. His worry proved baseless when a wave of royal blue flashed through Katz's glass double doors and there she was. She hurried over, hugged him, and sat down. Their waiter was in his early twenties. He had a shaved head, orange goatee, large silver-hoop earrings, and a big toothy smile interrupted by two missing incisors. The world was never short on interruptions. Cristina ordered coffee and a chocolate croissant. "So, Ollie, we are getting on in age, are we not?"

"Sad but true."

"How old are you now?"

"Jesus, Cristina, we don't even have your coffee yet. Sixty-two, same as Shuckle."

"Sixty-one."

"You don't look —"

"Lord, Ollie, don't say it, please. I sure as hell feel it." She laughed. "It seems to me how we feel ourselves to be is a far more accurate measure than how we look to the world around us. Shuckle never defined me by my looks, I must say."

Ollie laughed. "He told me the first time he saw you English became a second language."

The waiter brought the coffee and chocolate croissant and gave her his best and biggest interrupted smile. "Can I get you anything else?"

"No thank you."

For reasons he didn't fully understand, the waiter found himself overcome with a rather peculiar impulse. Without hesitation, he answered its call. He looked at Cristina, bowed full from the waist, straightened, turned, and walked away with his chin held high.

Cristina watched him. "Wasn't that beautiful!"

"Very," returned Ollie. "Shuckle calls those moments jewels. The jewels of life."

After a small bite of the croissant and a not so small sip of coffee, Cristina said, "They are jewels." She looked out the window and then back at Ollie. "When you see the finish line you realize things you'll never do, never accomplish. Not a pleasant reality held to certain lights, I know. But it's a reality that has its gifts, its jewels."

"Such as?"

"There's a lot to be said for clarity."

"You married still?"

"Quite a few years now. I have one child, Scott, named after my brother."

"I remember. And your husband's from Denmark."

"Victor Jenson. In his head he's still an aspiring painter, still thinks he's - "

"A reincarnation of Matisse."

"In reality he's an attorney. Estates mostly. He's from Helsingor, north a bit from Copenhagen."

"Are you happy?"

"He's a good husband and father." Cristina turned her head and looked out the window. There were tears in her eyes. "He still writes?"

"Of course. Writes and reads."

"I allow myself one stupid question in every conversation... He was so distrusting."

"No surprise. You get disowned by your mother a few weeks after your dad dies and wind up on the street, trust is hard to come by. He was fifteen. Shit. Lucky if you can spell trust after that. You know about that time the doctor called his mother, told her Shuckle had walking pneumonia and needed to be off the streets?"

"She hung up on him. I remember."

"He's not living in some myth when it comes to the end of your marriage, you know. He knows he was responsible.... Have you thought about seeing him?"

"There was so much extraordinary between us. He was the man of my dreams, even more than the man of my dreams, truth be told. It's been a long time since I thought about seeing him... His craziness didn't show right away. I suppose it rarely does. It was so clear he loved me."

"Still does."

"I know it."

"People are curious beings," said Ollie, catching the waiter's eye and tipping an imaginary cup of coffee to his mouth. Cristina nodded that she'd like another cup, and Ollie held up two fingers for the waiter. "Did you know Lord Byron was the first to mention Irish stew in writing?"

She laughed. "Where are you going with this? You and Shuckle, the two incorrigibles, the unpredictables of human discourse. No,

Ollie, I had no idea Lord Byron was the first to mention Irish stew. Pray tell."

"In his 1914 poem, the Devil's Drive - 'When he dined on some homicides done in ragoût, With a rebel or so in an Irish stew.'"

"God, how I've missed New York. Only here can a conversation go from Shuckle to Lord Byron and Irish stew."

The waiter with the interrupted smile refilled their coffees and, once again, bowed to Cristina. Cristina flashed a smile and nodded in acknowledgement. "What a sweetheart."

Ollie smiled. "I know trite might be hanging all over this, but I don't give a damn. We're all stews in our own right. All amalgams of many things. Sometimes you get a stew with six, seven ingredients, and let's say you like all the ingredients, except one. Something bitter, like bitter gourd. And when that taste hits your taste buds, you toss the whole stew away, if you've got any sense, because you know damn well you can't eat the food you love if you keep running into this horrible taste. In Shuckle's case, the bitter gourd was his temper, fear of abandonment, trouble trusting. It made a lot of him unreachable in any sustainable way. You never knew when the bitter gourd'd show up." Ollie moved the salt and pepper shakers closer to the window and then back to the center of the table. "That gourd's been gone a long time now, Cristina."

"Ollie, I don't see how it's possible for him to no longer be afraid of abandonment."

"No doubt. But what is possible is being free of the fear's decision-making power. On that front, he's been free for years now."

Shuckle Jones buttered and bagged two sesame seed rolls, filled his sixteen-ounce thermos with coffee, and headed out. Brown Dirt Dog saw him coming and wagged his tail. That the dog was always glad to see him had brought tears to Shuckle's eyes more than once. Again, he thought about letting the dog live with him, and again he set the thought aside.

Twenty minutes later they occupied a sunlit bench in Hamilton Fish Park. Shuckle gave one roll to the dog and kept one for himself.

Together, they enjoyed their morning fare. There is a comforting intimacy to sharing a meal, even between species. If Brown Dirt Dog curled up at Shuckle's feet, as he was wont to do, he always made sure his body was touching one of Shuckle's feet. Shuckle loved this. It was beautiful. He looked at the dog. "How's your roll?"

His cell phone buzzed, and the dog cocked his head when Shuckle Jones boogied on the bench a bit while he slapped at his pockets with both hands looking for the phone. It was his first cell phone in some time. It was not lost on him that the term cell phone was used less and less because it had been replaced with the goofy sounding, smartphone. Having the capacity to dial 9-1-1 at a moment's notice was not such a bad idea at his age, or any age for that matter. He just hoped he'd be able to make the call if he ever really needed to. He finally found and answered the phone. It was Ollie. Cristina would meet Shuckle for a cup of coffee at Katz's, tomorrow morning if he'd like.

It had happened.

All the years gone by and could his dream of being with Cristina again really be coming true? He knew this was not likely to be the case. What was he thinking? He got to his feet, balled up the bag and wax paper, and tossed them in the direction of a nearby garbage pail. "Back to the house," he told Brown Dirt Dog. When they were a few yards from the park's exit, Shuckle looked to his right and saw his father sitting on a park bench, smiling at him. "Wish me luck, Dad." His father nodded, and though his lips remained still, Shuckle heard him say: "I love you. Always remember that.   It will never go away."

For close to four years after their marriage ended, Cristina nixed any discussion of Shuckle in her presence. Savaged hearts and shattered dreams need distance. Now, nearly forty years later, she was meeting her first husband and soul mate for coffee. Yes, she felt love for her current husband, and no mother loved a son more than she loved hers. But there had been moments, more frequent of late, when she found herself pondering the reality of her marriage. Their marriage was comfortable. Neither felt any great desire to spend time together anymore. That said, they didn't dislike each other in the least. They could talk about the day's events over dinner with ease. They were like two portraits that have been hanging next to each other on the same wall for so many years no one really saw them anymore, nor could they see each other. On a level her conscious couldn't bring fully into view, she knew something was missing in her life, in her second marriage. That this was true grew increasingly clear as time passed. She'd agreed to see Shuckle again because she very much wanted to. He had never left her heart. Over the years she'd realized much of time's healing power rests on its uncanny ability to right-size things. And, as more time passed, she began to remember and, in a sense, rediscover Shuckle Jones. What she'd always known to be true was reaffirmed. She loved him. Soon, she would be in a conversation with him. Being in conversations together had been joyous experiences for both of them. So too the experience of being in each other's arms, and in each other's days.

Shuckle looked at his watch. Coffee with Cristina was in less than an hour. He was thoroughly showered, shampooed, shaved. He was wearing his best pair of jeans and a gray t-shirt with a picture of Beethoven on the front. He couldn't remember the last time he was this nervous, except maybe their June ninth wedding. Marrying an angel can be nerve-wracking, he remembered thinking. He grabbed his windbreaker and headed out the door. He was going to see Cristina, the woman who'd reached all of him with a completeness and depth unmatched by any other. His nerves calmed a bit when Brown Dirt Dog appeared at his side. "I'm going into the unknown," he told the dog. "I'm scared." His eyes wet up. He stopped walking, crouched down, and pet the dog. The dog pressed against him.

When they reached Katz's, he froze. There she was. She was sitting at a table by the window. Shuckle Jones knew that whatever happened, he would take the experience with him for the rest of his life. And then, she looked up and saw him. The world grew silent for both of them while each fully recognized the other and smiled. Shuckle Jones opened the door and stepped into the unknown.

Brown Dirt Dog stood in the lot next to Shuckle's building. The day was overcast, and the scent of rain was in the air. He read the ground with his nose and then lifted his head when the sky suddenly darkened. Seconds later, the sky was slit gold by lightning. Thunder quivered the earth. The dog looked over at Shuckle's kitchen window. The window guard and screen were gone. The window was open.

Heroes

There was nothing to say anymore, so he said nothing, knew this to be a wise choice. Wasting time was not victimless waste. It had taken him more than seventy-three years to understand this. This bothered him. It bothered him how things clear now, were not clear sooner.

He was tired of battering his mind to produce written words. That he thought and felt in words meant very little. He must have produced millions of those words over the years. Never wrote them down as much as he should have.

Sometimes Margaret would say she didn't understand his writing. When she said this, he'd change it. A mistake, he knew now. His written words were his progeny, their pattern reflected their upbringing. Changing them had been a disloyalty to himself, to his words, and, he'd realized, to Margaret.

He loved Margaret beyond words, believed in her. She was his wife, his hero. It pulverized his soul knowing he didn't tell her this until it was too late.

Now, it was morning and his coffee had cooled. He wanted another cup, a fresh cup, but his inclination covered only the want, not the action. This was early-morning porch time, light beginning to enter the day accompanied by bird songs, the bluster of Chickadees, Crows. God, how he loved listening to the birds.

Margaret used to sit with him in the morning. She drank tea. Lemon Zinger. One dollop of honey. When she smiled the moment became beautiful.

She died last fall, right in front of him, the two of them were sitting at the kitchen table. A sudden look of bewilderment came into her eyes as if she was suddenly confused, then a flinch, a stiffening, and she was gone. Just like that. Just like that. His first thought, you didn't finish your tea. His mind needed safe ground. He whispered, "You're my hero," and wept.

In the coffee shop mid-morning he could see Jake had a case of the grumbles. Merlene the waitress was late, again. "I should fire her," Jake said. He'd said this before, but everyone knew he'd never fire Merlene. Jake was in love with Merlene. Merlene lived with her ninety-two-year-old mother, Martha, a straw like lady a breeze might end.

Jake said, "I understand she's taking care of her mother, but a job's a responsibility, know what I mean?"

He did. He nodded.

"How's the coffee?"

"Little thin."

"Wouldn't be if Merlene made it."

"True."

Jake looked at him. Broke into a smile. "She's a sweetie, that Merlene."

"She sure is," he said, for the hundredth time.

He decided to walk home.

The slight uphill grade on Morton Street slowed him. He knew he was running out of energy. He paused in front of 62 Morton. Brownstone. Big Windows. Large oak doors. He'd made love with Jean Matthews many times in the back bedroom, up on the second floor. Her wet was delicious.

Her bedroom looked out over a well-gardened yard; a hammock marked its center. They were in their early twenties. Miracles were possible. Jean was kind. Life was good then, near nothing now. She'd married a stockbroker two days after her thirtieth birthday. Perhaps she'd stopped believing in miracles.

On the porch, late night now. The blue-black sky, star jeweled. Another day gone away.

Later that night, sitting on the edge of his bed, an open bottle of pills in his right hand. Four bottles of chilled wine cooler stood on the nightstand. Experts said alcohol helped. He shook six pills into his left hand. He drank them down with a couple of swallows from a wine cooler and poured out six more. He was on his way. He smiled. He missed Margaret.

Touching Hunger

Two weeks before she died Mary switched to day shift at Mookie's Diner. She and Mickey Quinn wanted more time together. Mickey was the day chef. He'd taken the job fourteen months earlier after moving back to the neighborhood. He'd tired of life in the big city; thirteen years was enough.

Life had not been easy for Mickey Quinn. He'd be the first to tell you much of the difficulty was his own doing. Mickey was like that. Honest. Straight forward. Said things in straight lines rather than leave you wondering. A rebellious streak got him fired from more than one job. (Six actually.) He'd never been a fan of authority. There'd been a brief stint of homelessness if one considers four months brief.

Mickey liked Mary straight away. Mary had her doubts. He seemed nice enough. She'd never seen a chef love his work as much as Mickey did. He was forever checking on the tables, making sure people were enjoying their meals, refilling coffees - sometimes to the wait staff's chagrin. On some occasions if people seemed down on their luck, not able to order as much food as maybe they'd like, Mickey'd come out of the kitchen moaning about having made too much lasagna or how had he been so stupid cooking up four more Philly cheese steaks than he needed. He'd give the food to those who looked like they needed it most, assuring them, while doing so, that they were doing him a favor by accepting it. He couldn't eat it all and if they didn't accept it, he'd have to throw the food out and - here he would dramatically cross himself and look sorrowfully up at the ceiling - his dear late mother would never forgive him. Mary liked how he watched out for their dignity, everybody's dignity, come to think of it. Including the wait staff, remarkably enough. Never treated them like servants, like there was nothing more to their lives than the fact they worked as waiters and waitresses. Still, she wasn't sure. First, she was beautiful. Formidably so by any measure. Her beauty got her attention from men (and some women) leaving her with the dispiriting task of figuring out if the person in question was talking to her or her looks.

With Mickey Quinn's straight forward way it didn't take her long to determine that, yes, he was, in fact, talking to her. But she wanted to be very careful. She'd made the wrong choice more than once. She'd done exactly that seven months earlier with tall, slender, deceitful Luke. Handsome Luke. A smile that could melt ice. The mouth that wore the smile spun falsehoods so elaborate they'd make any politician proud. Like other men of handsome stock, she'd slept with, he was a dud in bed. During the act, a disconcerting, pinched expression appeared on his face, making him look as if he was suddenly feeling nauseous, as opposed to being in the throes of, if not wonderful sex, pedestrian sex: recognizable, discernible, identifiable, sex. Anything, dear mother of God, except looking like you were fighting off the sudden onset flatulence.

Mickey signaled his interest in Mary by sending her flowers, anonymously at first. He paid his friend Rafael, a seventeen-year-old kid from the neighborhood, five bucks to deliver the flowers to Mary at the diner. Rafael made his money doing odd jobs in the neighborhood, sweeping up sidewalks in front of the stores in the warm weather, washing windows, shoveling snow in the winter, and delivering flowers. Rafael was under strict instructions to keep the identity of the sender secret.

Mickey'd bought the flowers from Herbert Slepoff, an old man with a Santa Claus beard who sold flowers twenty-four hours a day on the corner of Lilly Street and Box Avenue. The first time Rafael delivered the flowers to Mary she asked who they were from. "Got me, lady. Guess somebody likes you." Mary thanked him and gave him a five-dollar tip which led Rafael to tell Mickey he should keep sending flowers because it looked like it's working, the lady likes them a lot. Anyway, he thought, but did not say, she was beautiful and when she smiled his knees weakened. That, and who in their right mind gives up a ten-dollar gig if they don't have to?

Rafael lost his ten-dollar gig the day Mickey decided to deliver the flowers to Mary himself. He did not have to say a word, nor did she. But she did. Soft-smiling and wet-eyed: "You." And then the treasured first hug, where one sighs dreamily, happily, into the other arms, hearts and souls, bodies fully satiated.

Rafael was well liked in the neighborhood, known to be a good hard-working kid who gave his weekly earnings to his mother, never keeping more than five dollars for himself. His father walked out on them when Rafael was two months old. As far as Rafael was concerned, the sonuvabitch did not exist. Yes, his mother drank too much and let too many men like her for that one reason, but mother and son were close. No matter what their struggles, they were in it together.

Rafael attended evening GED classes twice a week, he told Mickey once, while the two of them were on the corner eating fresh apples Mr. Greenberg gave them for free because his oldest daughter Sylvia was engaged to be married and it was about time because Sylvia was pushing forty, thank you very much, and Mr. Greenberg wanted to know she was married, happy, and settled before he died. He had not been feeling so good lately, he told them. But he was smiling when he gave them the apples which was rare anyway because everybody knew what the numbers tattooed on his forearm meant. Morris Greenberg knew horror.

"When you get your GED then what?"

"My mother says you should make your dreams come true because if you don't, they stay in your head and next thing you know they're nothin' but memories."

"Smart woman."

Rafael nodded, quickly ate the core of the apple flicking the stem into the gutter. "How come you left the city?"

"Didn't work for me."

"It's expensive living there."

"Costs more'n dollars. You buy into the hype about the city so fast next thing you know you do not know who you are anymore. The city's the center of the world, summit of the universe. Most important place on planet earth. It is the, if you make it there you can make it anywhere crap, and, if you make it anywhere but there you are crap. That's how they get your money. Millions of dollars to live in brick fortresses without backyards 'less it's on the roof or something. You think if you move out, you're settling for second place, if that. You think you failed. You've been defeated by the big city. You weren't good enough. So, you stay. Most do anyway. Ever hear of H.L. Mencken?"

"Nope."

"Ballsy guy from Baltimore. Died in the fifties some time. Mencken said, "Nobody ever went broke underestimating the intelligence of the American public." The city's proof."

"Give me woods anytime."

"Me too."

"How'd you break out?"

"I don't remember when exactly, but at some point, I realized I was putting a whole lot of time and effort into being someone I am not, and never will be. Almost anything. It did not matter - actor, writer, anything'd make my name show up somewhere. You start thinking, fuck thinking, believing, if people didn't know your name you didn't exist! Like you're invisible."

"Like fame's the answer."

"Yeah. Fuck fame."

Rafael thought for a moment, bent down, tied his right sneaker, fingers deftly flashing. "So, what made you want to be a cook?"

"I'm walking home from this rehearsal on Grand Street. Winter. I see this old guy. Homeless guy. All balled up in a doorway. Store's closed, it's Sunday. He's wearing a fatigue jacket. Not camouflage like today, but the World War II kind - like my Dad actually." Mickey pauses, looks down the street, seeing nothing but his father in a World War II fatigue jacket. "Anyway... he's all balled up in the cold.

Poor guy was freezing. He's got this shopping cart with this one wobbly ass bent wheel next to him filled up with all kinds of shit he's been collecting. Bottles, cans, clothing, bags filled with scraps of paper. There's no way this guy's not hungry. So, I wake him up and ask him if he's hungry, and he says yeah, he's hungry. So, I ask him if he'd like me to get him something to eat, and he says yeah but he can't leave his cart by itself, and I get that, so I get us both some soup and buttered rolls and some coffee from a deli. I don't want him eating alone. Ends up we have a meal together."

"What'd you eat?"

"Soup and rolls, same as him."

"He knows you're equals."

Mickey smiles. "Fuck if he didn't used to be a high school math teacher. Dude was a mathematician; I'm talking real mathematician too. Turns out all those scraps of paper in those bags are all covered with figures and symbols."

"How'd he'd wind up homeless?"

"Didn't ask. Name was Mr. Reynolds. Alan Reynolds. Said all he wanted was to keep his stomach full, do his math problems, watch pretty girls, and think about his hero, this guy named Paul Erdős."

"Who?"

"Some famous mathematician, Hungarian man. There's some book about him called The Man who Loved Numbers. Mr. Reynolds loved him."

"You call him Mr. Reynolds?"

"What, you call your teachers by their first name?"

"Nope." Rafael smiles.

"So, Mr. Reynolds tells me he spends his days doing these math problems and thinking about Paul Erdős."

"And watching pretty girls."

"Told me he works on things called infinite series and set theory; shit I couldn't get on my best day. Looks like a different language. "

"You fed him?"

"Yup. That's when I knew."

Rafael, one eyebrow going up.

"Right then I knew I wanted to be a cook. Feed people. Nothing I can think of has more meaning than feeding someone."

"You die without it."

"Without it lots of things. You eat, you're taking care of yourself. You feed someone; you're helping them. There is something spiritual about it. Watching faces relax when they begin to chow down. Almost like they can rest for a moment, catch a break. With all the death and suffering in the world, man, no excuse but greed for people goin' hungry. I can't think of anything more honorable than feeding people. Life is good for me now, beyond what I ever hoped for. I cook food for people five days a week, Mary every day if she lets me. Take a break, she says, let me cook for you. She does too. Makes the best cheese omelet's I ever had. Cheddar. Little sprinkling of oregano. Life with her, man, it's gotta be one of the things makes people say heaven on earth."

"What happened to Mr. Reynolds?"

"Never saw him again. Walked by the same place next day he was gone."

"Ever wonder if he was real?"

"You mean did I imagine him?"

"Yeah."

"...Frequently."

It was three minutes past one in the afternoon when the first pain struck. Mary had just served Joe Montenegro his coffee. A portly, pasty man who daily stopped in for breakfast and lunch and regaled all who would (and would not) listen with stories of the good old days. (His good old days, anyway.) At seventy-three the perpetually wheezing retired bookkeeper was proud of the fact his father, the late Giuseppe Montenegro, had been a milkman. Not milk person, thank you very much.

Joe Montenegro would snap at anyone who dared to correct him and use what they stupidly thought was the politically correct word, milk person. Bull. As low on the totem pole of success as he might've been in the eyes of some, his father had been the real thing, the real deal. He had been a milkman.

"A milkman was about a lot more than just milk. (Insert sir, madam, or friends.) Poppa would bring full bottles of fresh milk and pick up the empties. This was a certainty. Life needs certainty. He'd bring his customers cream, cheese, eggs, butter, even soda pop! It is a stain on this country that the nurturance of simplicity is no more, a stain as sure as I'm sitting here. And what is life now, I ask you? (He never gave his answer, and one was never offered.) People staring into those so-called smart phones and iPads. Can you think of a name that screams self-absorbed louder than that product's name? I think not."

Joseph Montenegro was in the middle of providing his milkman monologue to Pastor James Winston of the local Methodist Church. Mary came by, refilled their coffees, turned to go, dropped the metal coffee pot on the floor, and grabbed at her chest. Clenched in pain on the floor Mary inexplicably found herself watching a thin rivulet of coffee leaking from the coffee pot and wondered if it would reach the base of the counter. "Jesus," she whispered, exhaling.

"You okay, kid?"

"My chest." Again, clutching. "This isn't right. I'm wrong with me. Mickey!" Her mind shadow swimming in memories, soft patches then sudden arcs of color, pulsing, and need, so much need. Thinking, Mickey? Yes, God, the pain, can I remember, please, that lovely thing he did, his car breaking down, the state trooper giving him a ride home. Mickey baking a cake and bringing it to the trooper's barracks three days later... Oh, God, Mickey, not now. She was sick with the flu, the knock on the door, then the key. Mickey, thank God. In he came with the best chicken soup she had ever had in her life. He made her tea with real honey, not the dead honey sold in stores. "You're magic with food," she said. He kissed her, flu, and all. He kissed her. Pain surging. Mickey, please!

Mary on the floor behind the counter, unconscious now, sweat soaked. Mookie holding her head, weeping, Pastor James Winston's lips moving in prayer. The ambulance arrives. Fifty-seven minutes later in the emergency room Mary is pronounced dead.

Three months later.

Mickey avoids all music. Melody tears holes in his chest. He does not walk down certain streets. Memories everywhere. Every street, heartbreak. When he did walk it was in the park, shoulders hunched, head bowed, expecting another blow at any moment. Another would kill him. (A welcome event.) Sometimes sitting on the grass against a tree he wishes he could be a little boy again, start all over. Why would God kill a young woman with a heart attack?

It has been weeks since anyone has seen him. He had his phone disconnected. Did not answer the door. After the burial he never went back to the diner. He just vanished. Disappeared. Mookie told people he always had a job at the diner, but after weeks went by and nobody heard from him, nobody said a thing when he hired another day chef. Rafael stopped in from time to time, made eye contact with Mookie, one of the servers, heads wagged no. No one had seen him.

Mickey's landlady said he had moved out, no forwarding address. "He was heartbroken sad," she told Rafael. "Sometimes a body just knows when enough is enough." Now Rafael was scared. Not that he thought Mickey would kill himself, but, then again, it would not be the first time he had been wrong about people. Hell, Billy Winston won more than $18,000 in a poker game at Sal's Chimney Room one night, went home and put a gun in his mouth. Note said he wanted to go out a winner. Fucking people. You just never know.

Early morning bone cold tired on a bench, a pulsing ache, fragmented thoughts, somewhere in the thinking dark, the day's first birds flipped pastel jewels of sound into the air, flickers of life. He tried and failed to grab onto them, sing back in return, call out, but there was too much ache, and, for some reason, he could not move his mouth. Maybe he was still sleeping, or this was death.

The birds again. Again, he struggled. Then a familiar voice in a whisper from far away called his name. The ache now begins to fade, the flicker of bird songs farther away now. Good, quiet. Let go. Let it all go.

Then, again, the familiar voice in a raised whisper. "Mickey. Yo, Mickey."

He was in motion. Rocking now. Someone was rocking him. His eyes open. Rafael is looking down at him, tear-filled eyes, smiling. "Hey, we miss you." Rafael helps him onto a park bench, takes off his coat, wraps it around Mickey's shoulders, pulls it closed in front. Mickey nods, still unable to speak. Not yet. Speaking means, return. Come back. Not yet.

"You hungry?"

Mickey nods.

"Me too. I've got food in the car. I'll be right back."

One And The Same

Russell's ass hits the floor as soon as he lays down on the bed. No springs. Just a mattress on a metal frame. He says, "Fuck."

Royal fares better. His bed holds up (somewhat) under his slender frame.

Russell again says, "Fuck."

"That's the truth," Royal returns, laughing at Russell's v-shaped posture. "Put the mattress on the floor."

Russell struggles to his feet, says, "Fuck," and the mattress hits the floor with a thud. "It is on the floor. Village Plaza Hotel my ass."

Royal says, "You see a bathroom anywhere?"

"Down the hall right side."

"I'll be back."

"Fuck."

The bathroom is covered in slime, mildew, specks of feces on the toilet lid, cobwebs across the ceiling, a filthy glazed window, and at least two battalions of cockroaches crawling over everything. Royal mutters, "Mother of God," backs out, closes the door, leans his forehead against the damp cool of the smudged white bathroom door, inhales, thinks, Let me just get this over with, do it, get this shit over with, which was, after all, the purpose of his bathroom trip in the first place. He had to take a shit, though the phrase always perplexed him seeing how you don't take a shit, you leave a shit, so who on earth came up with take a shit? Doesn't matter now. All he knows is he has to shit.

He goes back into the bathroom and does exactly that. Eyes clenched, squatting over the filthy toilet teeming with roaches, a moving black veil over porcelain, he releases a puffing fart and shits.

Back in the room Russell asks, "How'd it go?"

"Million roaches in there. Disgusting. They're everywhere. Mother of God, I thought they'd crawl up my ass."

"Fuck."

The two boys lay back on their beds and stare up at the ceiling, the least disturbing view available. Now they know the only remotely classy thing about the Village Plaza Hotel is its name. In truth it's a dive off Washington Square Park on Washington Square Place. But it's 1972 and they are in Greenwich Village, a reputed haven for artists, musicians, writers, land of lofty dreams, boundless sexual freedoms (they hope), and creativity. They don't know it yet, but it's also a haven for poverty, drugs, realities made less obvious to the boys by their misguided belief that Greenwich Village is a world that will enlighten them, grow them to greatness. They don't know it yet, but their minds are riding the heady slipstream of pipe dreams, believing their very presence in Greenwich Village has given them a kind of artistic and sexual standing. They don't know it yet, but poverty breeds crushing heartbreak and often its sibling, the choking dysfunction of loneliness. For the moment they are utterly wedded to their pipe dreams, vulnerable.

Russell is the writer and lover of books and Royal is fixed on possible and impossible sexual adventures with men and women.

The fact Russell is straight, and Royal is bisexual has no particular meaning to either boy. They are the same age, seventeen, and they've been friends since they were four and the difference in their sexual proclivities has no bearing on their experience of each other, save for an amusing tongue-in-cheek exchange they have from time to time, Royal saying, "I can choose from everyone," to which Russell says, "That means every person on planet earth can tear your heart out, bro. Least I just have to worry about half," to which Royal says, "Touché brother."

"We need some girls," says Russell, staring at the ceiling and peeling off his socks.

"Bare feet on this floor?"

Russell says, "Fuck," and puts his socks back on.

"Think the radio works?" Royal points at a battered white radio on top of a four-drawer bureau shoved in the far corner of the room.

Russell pads over, clicks it on, and the room fills with the sounds of the Rolling Stones' Tumbling Dice.

"It's Mick," Royal says.

"Mucus lips."

"Common he's cute."

"Please."

"And sexy."

"You got too much cholesterol in your diet, bro."

"What's cholesterol got to do with it?"

"About as much as Mick has to do with sexy."

Royal Cleaves is rail thin, but strong. He stands six-feet two-inches tall, has a narrow face, full lips, narrow nose, blue eyes a bit too wide set for his face, and long thin brown hair that seems to dance with his every move. He was raised by his mother, Alice Cleaves. They are very close. His father abandoned them when Royal was only three months old. He is an only child. For Royal, his father is a cloudy dream, dark and murky, unreachable, indefinable, and even worse, not real.

Alice Cleaves has been an administrative assistant for the same plumbing supply company in Spring Valley for more than 30 years: Perfect Pipe Plumbers on Main Street. She is a mother comfortable accepting her son for who he is and equally comfortable at encouraging him to be just that. Over the years Alice Cleaves has encountered her fair share of criticism over the fact her son is openly bisexual. School teachers, principals, a local shopkeeper, Horace Grimply of Grimply's Diamond Dust Bakery, and, of course, members of the clergy. In particular a plump little priest named Father Horatio Muffin who more than once wailed to her in drippy nasal tones that the poor boy could be cured of "this here bisexual disease" if he'd just turn his life over to God. Alice Cleaves had too merciful a heart to say she believed it was Father Muffin who needed the curing. She didn't think very much of his God either.

Royal was, in the clearest light, an inconsistent student through grammar school and high school. He loved the intricacies and mysteries of math and science, couldn't care less about English, found history boring, deplored gym, and saw homeroom as a time to contemplate the sexual possibilities of his classmates.

Royal Cleaves, eighty-seventh in his graduating class of 183 students, knew that before he moved on to college, if he moved on to college, there were certain things he wanted to experience. All required living in New York City, Greenwich Village to be specific. He had a curiosity about the S&M Clubs he'd heard about in the West Village - the Anvil and the Eagle's Nest. He wanted to dress in loud flowing colors, wrap silk scarves around his neck and let them flow gloriously behind him like mellifluous dreams. He wanted to wear eye make-up and lipstick and, if the mood struck him, heels. More than once when his mother wasn't home, he put a pair of her heels on. His legs were long and slender like hers and he knew they were as beautiful as those on any woman he'd ever seen. He would, he hoped, find a sanctuary for himself in Greenwich Village, a community that accepted difference as the norm. There is relief in acceptance and - real or imagined - a sense of safety.

Russell's story was different but the same as things often are. Abandoned in a Hell's Kitchen alley early one October morning just days after his birth he is found and rescued by Simon Goldfein, a pale and sweaty newspaper delivery man who pulled his truck into a back alley that morning so he could continue reading the latest Mickey Spillane novel, "Kiss Me Deadly". With the engine off and window a couple of inches for air, Simon Goldfein, called Stony by friends and family, hears a baby crying. Stony finds the baby in an open garbage pail wrapped in a faded blue flannel shirt. When he lifts the crying baby into his arms the shirt falls open revealing a naked struggling baby boy. When he covers the baby back up the baby stops crying, coos, and, to Stony's amazement, smiles. Stony smiles back at him. "Not the way to start a life little man."

With the newborn wrapped in his arms, Stony drives straight to the New York Foundling Hospital on 68th Street and Third Avenue. Stony remembers reading that the hospital opened in 1869 to rescue babies abandoned after the Civil War. As they approach the hospital Stony realizes he will cry when he hands the baby over to hospital staff. He hopes he can hold back the tears, at least until he is back behind the wheel, one of only two places he feels some sense of control over his life, behind the wheel and reading a book. When Sister Emma Luther takes the baby boy from his arms something inside of him breaks. He wonders what the baby boy he's secretly named Lincoln feels. Back in his truck he breaks down and sobs. The Mickey Spillane book had fallen out of the truck when he'd gone in with the boy. He leaves without noticing it on the ground, half of its worn pages submerged in a small muddy puddle. He'll never remember reading the first thirty-two pages of the book, much less the book itself. He will always remember Lincoln.

While Stony never learns who adopts the boy, he does get a letter six weeks later telling him the boy has been placed with a good family.

He will never know the boy was adopted by a father who loves him and a mother who doesn't. He will never know the boy is named Russell Vincent Falter. He will never know about the tragedy that strikes the boy's life when he is fifteen, his father struck down unexpectedly by a heart attack and his mother, sixteen weeks later, placing him in reform school, telling the court the boy is out of control, crazy even. He will never know that when the boy is released from reform school one year later, he is disowned by his mother and finds himself homeless on the very streets from which he, Stony, rescued him just days after his birth. He will never know, but would be truly comforted if he did, that the boy's father introduced the boy to the world of books and, like Stony, books will provide the boy with a place of refuge for the rest of his life.

When Stony drives away from the hospital and for the first time in his life he feels no sense of control behind the wheel.

When Russell's father dies unexpectedly the boy's ability to feel safe in the world dies with him. And while reform school is anything but enjoyable, he discovers a welcome kind of anonymity there. Everyone is known by their last name. Hey Falter, whatcha doin'? Hey Falter, wanna play some ball? Hey Falter, shut the fuck up, ya gotta snore so fuckin loud? You're a fuckin' kid for Chrissakes!

While in reform school he thinks about his father a lot. When he was with his father, he could safely be himself. He was free of judgment and criticism and, most of all, free of being told he's too intense. His mother repeatedly told him his intensity marked him as deeply flawed and, worse still, mentally ill. He still believes his intensity means something wrong with him mentally. He believes intensity is an illness, something to be fought, avoided, denied. He thinks too about how much he loved life before his father died. Now he's not so sure. The jury's out on that one.

After he is released from reform school, he is sent to a half-way house in the city. His mother makes it clear he no longer has family. She does not want him back. He is alone and on his own. Period. End of story.

One day he gets into a fight with another boy at the half-way house and each is given the same choice - go back to reform school and serve out your eighteen-month sentence or hit the streets. The other boy chooses to serve the four months remaining on his sentence, Russell hits the streets, not realizing that what feels like choosing freedom will, in truth, lock him in a cell of merciless isolation.

It takes him four months to get off the streets, doing so, finally, by getting a job as a laborer for a hard-drinking mason named Tony Rizzo after convincing Rizzo he'd always dreamed of a life building with bricks and floating concrete. He finds a place to stay landing a room with a single mother of two named Joan. Joan is kind to Russell. In exchange for babysitting her two children in the evening, three-year-old Sasha, and two-year-old Terrence, she waives the rent.

Joan drinks too much in the evening and when she does, she becomes sexually aggressive, at times disrobing completely and climbing into bed with Russell. Russell is always gentle redirecting her, getting her into the kitchen where he cooks up a pot of coffee for them both and, in the morning, or later the next day, Joan is always thanks Russell for not having taken advantage of her.

The boy's room is hideous. Stained wallpaper with barely discernible floral patterns (Daisies maybe?) peels off the wall like sunburned skin. The linoleum's behavior mirrors that of the wallpaper. There are two windows looking out over the street. One slams gunshot shut when Royal lifts it and let's go thinking it will stay while the other, when lifted, wedges itself stuck before it can be nudged loose and closed, one frame cracking in the process. The entire room reeks of Lysol and both boys wonder what smells they'll encounter once the Lysol smell wears off.

Looking out the window Russell says, "Wouldn't it be nice if two girls just showed up?"

Royal smiles. "I can feel a line forming right now."

And while one might not put this or any of Royal's remarks for that matter on the summit of prescience, there is a knock on the door exactly ten minutes later. Ever the protector, Russell answers the door. He is stunned. Standing before him are two girls. Both look to be in their mid-twenties, both have long hair parted in the middle. One girl's hair is completely and utterly blue. The other girl's hair is red on one side of the part and purple on the other side. Russell decides they use the same hairdresser.

"Hi," Blue Hair says.

"Hey," Russell says.

Royal calls out, "Who?"

"Two girls, bro."

"Can we come in? Are you busy?" Purple Red Hair now. "We heard you guys moved in and wanted to welcome you. Mind? We live here too."

Royal at the door now says, "Not at all. Come in."

There is not a lot of talk at first, the two girls look around the room taking it in as if they'd never seen a room like this which Royal thinks can't possibly be true because they're staying in the same hotel and he can't, for the life of him, imagine there's a wide range in room quality. After they've given the room the once over, they look at each other and, as if on cue, giggle.

"We like your room," Purple Red Hair says.

It doesn't take long for them to say, with a directness that brings both boys up short, that they'd like to have sex with Royal but not with Russell. I mean they like Russell and all but he's too manly and Royal has an effeminate quality they like and would Russell mind very much going for a walk? Maybe a long walk? Two hours maybe?

And so it is that Russell finds himself walking into Washington Square Park a few minutes later baffled by the fact he'd just been rejected by two girls because he's too manly. Surrounded by people Russell feels alone. Hands shoved deep in the pockets of his jeans he walks through a cloud of marijuana, a scent he recognizes and likes, and a cloud of pungent incense, a scent he doesn't recognize or understand. The lacy sounds of guitar playing fill the air. A tambourine plays offbeat, a tipsy Harlequin sound. Russell slows and stands at the edge of a small crowd listening to an elderly tone-deaf woman wrapped in a large red shawl singing Row-row-row your boat at the top of her ancient smoke-stained lungs. The crowd applauds affectionately, aiming kindness at the old lady who has found a way to give herself permission to live her life her way, or so it seems to Russell's young eyes.

"Sing another one, Martha!" the crowd calls out. At the sound of applause and encouragement Martha begins singing Mary Had a Little Lamb and her audience joins in. Russell joins in too using the singing-whisper voice used by those who sing in fear. One of the young men singing along turns and seems to look right at Russell. Grateful for the connection right down to his nearly buckling knee, Russell smiles and nods in acknowledgment. The young man's expression remains unchanged, his eyes black, his mouth singing with the others, and while he continues to look right at Russell, the young man does not see him. Feeling more alone and invisible than ever, Russell falls silent, turns, and walks out of the park.

Soon he is watching a hard fought basketball game on a well-lit fenced-in court off of West Third Street. It's a full size court. The game churns away, a kind of modern cage match. Players of all colors and backgrounds, some shirtless, others not, muscles sweaty in swirling speed, amazing skill. Some with fros, some with long hair, others close cropped, every player oblivious to all things but the game, the power of their focus not lost on Russell, the brotherhood of it all, family. As the tears come, he turns and heads up Sixth Avenue.

Swish!

On the corner of 8th Street and Sixth Avenue he stops at Nathan's and orders an orange drink filled with pulp and carbonation. He is uncomfortable, out of place, sure the couple with long hair standing four feet away are talking about him. What's he doing here? He doesn't belong here, not in Greenwich Village. We're artists. He's nothing. Look at him. The man smiles at him. Russell doesn't believe the smile. He thinks the man feels sorry for him, pities him. Pity is nothing more than emotional vomit and Russell knows it. To escape the stench, he looks across the avenue and for the first time since leaving the room, he smiles. Across the street is a large newsstand filled with newspapers, magazines, journals. It has a battered green awning with the words International News 405 6th Avenue on it in faded white letters.

Russell puts his drink down and charges across the street, not hearing the horns blaring at his recklessness. Under the awning now he sees newspapers from all over the world. He sees racks and wooden platforms filled with every kind of journal and magazine imaginable. The journals draw his attention. They are thicker and hold the welcome promise of longer periods of escape. There are journals on writing, philosophy, sex, science, poetry, politics, dreams, hopes, memories, fantasies, sports, geography, history and then, in the corner of one of the racks, he sees the Metropolitan Chess Journal with the title Chess Giants in large bold letters on the cover. He takes it down from the rack and sees it has games played by Emmanuel Lasker, José Raúl Capablanca, Alexander Alekhine, Bobby Fischer and there, right there, his favorite chess player ever, Sammy Reshevsky. This journal actually has games played by Sammy Reshevsky!

Sure, maybe the Cuban great Capablanca, considered by many the most naturally gifted chess player, and Alekhine, Lasker, well, they were greats too, perhaps even greater than Reshevsky, and Fischer, deadly good Fischer who may turn out to be the best of them all. But to Russell's mind a player's chess style is like a writer's writing style. It reflects the person's character. When he used to play out Reshevsky's games with his father they knew they were spending time with a friend.

Looking at Reshevsky's name on the cover, Russell realizes he doesn't have enough money. He's down to two dollars after the orange drink. The journal is two-fifty.

The newsstand proprietor is a sweaty heavyset grizzle-faced man wearing an old white t-shirt and dark slacks with a green waist apron filled with change. He seems oblivious to the cool temperature. A lit cigarette sticks out of the corner of his mouth like an appendage. When he talks, it bobs up and down, a pale white flailing baton. His countenance is hurried, grumpy, impatient.

Russell says, "Think you'll have one of these chess manuals tomorrow?"

To the boy's surprise, the proprietor's countenance softens. He smiles. "Like chess, do you?"

"My father taught me. This has some of Reshevsky's games in it. He's my favorite player."

"You don't want to buy it now?"

"I'm a little short."

"How short's a little short."

"Fifty cents."

"You know what the en passant move is?"

"Yeah. If someone moves their pawn two spaces on first move and passes through a space controlled by one of your pawns, you can move into the passed square and take it."

"I'm impressed. Your Dad taught you well."

"What time you open tomorrow."

"Twenty-four seven, kid. This is my world."

"See you in the morning then." Russell turns to leave.

"Gimme a buck."

Russell turns back.

"It's yours for a buck."

"I got two bucks"

"No, never leave a man penniless, bad omen, kid. You gimme a dollar, I give you the journal, the deal is made. You get rich and famous someday, coffee's on you."

The boy hands over a dollar and the proprietor hands him the journal.

"Thanks, mister."

"Tommy."

"Thanks Tommy."

"My pleasure kid. You gotta name?"

"Russell."

"Good name, kid."

Russell standing on the southeast corner of 6th Avenue and 10th Street is looking across street at a castle, a Victorian gothic structure with some kind of turret and tower on top with a clock on it that's lit by a light strategically placed out of view. The building is red brick with limestone trim. Russell thinking, A castle in the middle of a city.

He crosses the street and stands at the foot of the castle steps. He looks up, trying to see the turret and tower. He feels cold. A raspy male voice says, "Lost?"

The voice comes from the top of the steps. Russell sees no one there, only a dark motionless spectral shape on top of the stairs. Again, the voice, but this time a statement, not a question. "You're lost." Again, the voice comes from the top of the stairs and again he looks and again no one is there, only the dark motionless spectral shape.

Russell walks slowly up the steps, unsure, hesitant, aware of nothing in the world now but his movement, the motionless spectral figure reveals itself to be nothing more than a large pile of rags.

Russell stops, listens. Someone is breathing. Leaning forward he realizes it's the pile of rags. At the very moment this fact registers the pile of rags says, "Hello boy." It is instantly not lost on the boy that he is in a moment that should, but doesn't, scare him; the raspy voice is kindness embracing.

"I didn't realize you were a person."

"Few do," says the rags. "You like libraries?"

"Excuse me?"

"Do you like libraries?"

"I like books."

"I know that" says the rags. "What's your view of libraries."

"I like them too."

"Good. You're in the right place. This is a library."

"Looks like a castle."

"It's actually the Jefferson Market Branch of the New York City Public Library, born the Third Judicial Courthouse around 1833."

"Born?"

"All things are born. It's the arrogance of our species to think otherwise."

Russell nods, not realizing he is leaning down to get a closer look at the pile of rags.

"I do have a face, my boy. Like to see?"

Russell straightening nods.

There's a shift and a twist and an arcing flame of fabric and out pops a shaggy gray head with wild thick curly gray hair and a thick curly gray beard to match. Looking at Russell from within the thick and swirling gray are a pair of remarkably clear dark brown eyes crowned with two dark eyebrows. And then, a smile appears, a smile that lights the night and before he knows it, Russell is smiling too, thinking the shaggy gray man's smile has got to be one of the most beautiful smiles he has ever seen and without realizing he is doing it, he sits down on the top step next the old man. He is not cold anymore.

Russell says, "You're right, by the way."

"You're lost."

"Yeah. Lost the whole family actually."

"How?"

"Dad died, few weeks later, Mom puts me in reform school. I get out, that's it. No more family."

"She sounds like a sad lady."

"Controlling lady."

"Controlling is a garment of sadness. What's the magazine?"

"It's a chess journal with all kinds of games you can play out. It's my favorite game."

"Mine too. How'd you learn?"

"My Dad started teaching me when I was four. We'd play for hours. He gave me a book called "The First Book of Chess" by Joseph Leeming. The cover had a picture of the white king with black and red chess squares in the background. I remember my Dad said it was published in 1953, same year I was born."

"Still have the book?"

"Nope. Wish I did though. I'm pretty sure my mother threw it out. Threw most of his stuff out, except for his clothes. I think she gave them to the church or something."

"But the book was yours."

"Same thing."

A pause.

"How old are you?"

"Seventeen."

"Awfully young to be alone in the world."

Russell smiles, somehow finding it comforting that the shaggy gray man can tell he is alone in the world. For a moment constant companion fear is gone. And for the first time since he began his walk in the chilly night, he feels relaxed and safe.

They pause now, people watching. Every kind of person imaginable. Well dressed, poorly dressed, hardly dressed, attire like costumes, though Russell thinks everyone wears a costume whether they realize it or not.

"Tell me about your father?" The question asked in a soft gentle voice.

Russell knows he has no chance of describing his father in a way that would let anyone really know, even this shaggy gray man, how precious and kind and loving and beautiful his father was. He can say, He was my best friend, and He was the greatest gift life has ever given me and I would give up the rest of my life in an instant to hug him one more time and still not come close to truly describing the depth of love that lived between father and son. And so, Russell said the only thing a boy who loved his father more than life could say. "He was everything."

The shaggy gray man nodded his head, his face in gentle smile. "What was his name?"

Russell smiles. "Sam."

"Well now, wouldn't you know it."

"Know what?"

"That's my name. Sam."

Russell looks into the warm brown eyes that shine at him from within the swirls of gray, wondering, could it be? His young mind taking him to the kind of hopes the passage of time kills or hides in most. Could his father somehow be inhabiting this man's body just for now to visit his son to let him know everything will be all right?

Maybe he didn't die! The casket was closed. Russell never saw him dead. Russell remembering standing at the head of his father's casket in the Hugh E. White Funeral Home. His hand ever so gently clasping the corner, fiercely protective. People passing by, floating, nameless, faceless, except for his Uncle Jimmy who hugged him and meant it. Jimmy, his father's younger brother by one year, one of Russell's favorite people ever. Yet everyone else is nameless, faceless, passing by without moving. Russell thinking, Daddy, I won't leave you, not ever. I'm here. You're not alone, we are one and the same.

And now this shaggy gray man in rags with the same name. Sam. A simple warm name. Huggable. Believable. Could this Sam in some way out of the reach of understanding really be my father visiting me, here in this crazy city with too much of everything? Tears came.

Sam makes a rustling sound rooting around in his rags and withdraws a plaid thermos. He unscrews the plastic cup on top of the thermos and places it on the ground next to him. He pours coffee into the plastic cup, picks it up, and offers it to Russell. "You'll feel better." Russell drinks. The coffee soothes. "How long ago did he die?"

"Little over a year."

Sam looks up at the sky as it starts to rain. "It's kind of magical really. The rain falls, and it's like this veil in front of us. A fourth wall. Makes a space like this feel more like a nest. Something comforting about it. You feel protected. One of nature's hugs if you will."

Russell drinks more coffee, watches the rain. "You're right. It's comforting."

"Try not to miss the moment you're in."

"The moment I'm in?"

"It's the only place you have to be."

There is a stillness now as the two sit side by side on the top step. The shaggy gray Sam swaddled in his swirl of many colored rags. Russell only inches away, plastic cup with a feather of steam, denim jacket, flannel shirt, jeans, sneakers, cap. Silence now. People shadows passing by hunched and hurried in the rain. To where? Russell wonders. Doesn't matter, Sam knows. And then, as if on cue, the rain stops. It doesn't fade or halt. It just stops. The last breath of something. Nature's heartbeat.

"And so, what now, my boy?" Sam asks.

"I don't know. I want to write, meet someone maybe."

"What do you want to write?"

"Stories, I think. I'm out of my league here though."

"The city?"

Russell nods.

"Not true. The city's just more people in one place. More people, more noise, more confusion, more everything. Too much of everything frankly."

"More talent."

Sam smiles. "Get out of your way."

"I know."

"Most never get out of their own way. Look around, almost everybody's trying to be someone they're not." Here Sam looks up at the dark clear sky. "Why do you think there's so much sadness? All that wasted energy. People trying to reinvent themselves all the time rather than be who they are. Your father wanted you to be you."

"How do you know?"

"Any son who says his father is everything had a father who loved his son. Not somebody else, his son. Your father loved you, the who you are you. I think your father's deepest wish is that you be you, the son he loved. Still loves."

"Do you have kids?"

"A son. Just out of my reach, but a son." And here Sam's shaggy gray head turns and faces the boy, looks directly at Russell. "Be you."

They hold each other's look for a moment. "I'll try," Russell says, suddenly overcome with sleepiness. "I will."

Sam smiles as he watches the boy lean against his shoulder and drift off into sleep. The boy is still sleeping when the light of morning makes its first appearance of the day. He is still sleeping an hour later when foot traffic has begun to pick up. It is only when a familiar voice says, "What're you doing sleeping up there?" that he slowly wakes up. "I was worried about you," Royal says coming up the steps. "What're you doing here?"

"Sam and I have been here all night."

"What Sam?"

Russell turns to the shoulder he was leaning on and finds there is nothing there but a pile of rags under a sign against the wall that reads, Please Leave Clothes for Homeless. Something inside of him stills, "I must've been dreaming."

"Let's go get some coffee."

Russell picks up his chess journal and stands up. Nodding towards the ground Royal says, "Don't forget your book." Russell looks down and sees "The First Book of Chess" by Joseph Leeming with the white king on the cover and black and red chess squares in the background.

Paper Clips

The paper clip was on the sidewalk, a foot from the curb cut. No rust. New arrival. Alone. He picked it up and put it in his pants' pocket. It was safe now. He felt better. The paper clip would have a life. He had papers everywhere, some in stacks. Pads, notebooks of every walk of life, composition style, hardback sketchbook style, moleskin, spiral. They were everywhere. Papers clipped and stapled. Papers in need of clipping and stapling. The paper clip would have a life. That's how he felt about it. It felt good.

There were quiet parts of himself, perhaps not quiet, as much as private. Coming down the stairs the previous morning he'd whispered, "Sorry little one," to the dead body of a fly, alone on the floor, below the windowsill. A life all gone.

Outside, he thinks of it still. In that dwelling we call the human mind, filled with rooms he'd found one room in which he could quietly privately acknowledge to himself alone, his instinct for noticing something about himself he was actually fond of. He cared.

Poems

A Good Thing

If we
in this world
would listen
with and honest ear
then I would hope
that you would do
the same for me.

I do
with a gratitude sure
remember your goodness
to me and I
with an honest tongue
do thank you
in the purest sense
that life will allow me.

In time
there are few
that we can say
are living deep
within us
and I
do claim this of you
for me.

I do way
with the proudest chin
that I have known you
and no matter the consequence it
for me
is a good thing

On The Relaxin'

I was bothering no one I was merely reading
Out loud this thing I'd set down a short time earlier
Swearda God I wasn't bothering a soul
Had the damned t's crossed and I's dotted
Don't believe I was dangling
Too many participles
I was just an innocent man
Just hanging out

On the relaxin'

There I was in mid sentence stroll
Eyes meeting those attending
When slam pow screech shit
There you were
And I slipped into the pool
There was no footin' left
Cause there you were
Soft-eyed lookin straight back

On the relaxin'

I sucked up my forty-one year old gut
Broke free of a conversation
braved my knee-buckling fear sweat
And with hands shoved in pockets
Invited you to coffee with us
So now you get really slippery and say okay
I'm outside cool saying - Certainly
While inside the boy says - Serious?

On the relaxin'

Soon we discovered nestled mornings
Your very hot tea and my coffee
Sipped during the crackle rasp
Of newspaper pages turning
Putting all on hold here and there
Making room for the kiss
And the skin to skin
Don't let the day begin embrace

On the relaxin'

Life seems to be with you now
We are fast growing heart joined
Learning our landscapes
And you like my words and I
Like your magic full length
Around me in gentle form
The scent of peace is in the air
We are the healing newborn

On the relaxin'

I see more sun in the day now
The movement of the lake outside
My window seems even smoother
And even the coffee tastes better
And who the hell knows
Maybe there is a God
Just look at you in cotton folds
Smiling at me

On the relaxin'

Distance

I
born of you,
a clouded secret
I'll never know -
      Distance.

We,
knew a moment,
ours alone,
ours shortened -
      Distance.

Mother,
you I love,
never forgetting,
quietly in -
      Distance

July 26, 1984

Write On

This the pathway to
Words touch tender touch
My page and my hand
Pen sends friendship
To your wordsmith self
Our camaraderie
Write on
People
Smile

Life Electric

I get to hug you again
Coming incandescent through the door
Pumping life electric singing
Whitman's barbaric YAWP and
My hand hugging her
Waist through the soft cloth
Registers the moment welded
Full complete never to be
Forgotten and Oh God
I thought (hoped!)
She was going to kiss me
Melting

Jan. 26, 1997

Borders

I am thinking of you out there
Quietly in tune thinking
I love you silently hoping

In moments shadowed in quiet
Tender Believing that truth prevails
Under peeled down skin
I am stepping in rhythm tumbling confidence

Beyond my weary borders

For JCH

Bagpipes

Always bagpipes

I can only reach you touch you here
On this thin piece of wood called paper
It is the only place left for us
And this saddens me truly

And you wouldn't believe me
Calling to you off this page
And this is why I don't call
To say I will always love you
Greatly grateful and never
Regret that glorious September day
And o your magic laugh
Always bagpipes

For PGK & VBK

For John Steinbeck

Meet you on the crest
Of a striding sentence

Maybe we can hug
A noun together

Or thank a verb

Or even give a chuckle
Of appreciation
To the tempting pull
Of an adjective

Say hi to Charley for me

Word Shine

Words shine for a ramble
on this page with their
rhythms set free
they walk stride skip
carrying you along
for how long
we've yet to see
remember to breathe

She Turns Words Loose

She
turns words
loose in me
gentle soft travelers
sent across all of her
being in deep amatory
movement wandering her
sweet configurations in velvet
darkness feather tasting undulating
shapes I'd believe unreal
if I wasn't
awake.

Quiet

Quiet is sweet sound
Healing me to my depths
All the way through
Comfort

In All Times

In all times
And in all lives
There are moments
Filled with the
Sincerest intimacy
You and I shared
Such moments
And I thank you
And love you
For those times

Written August 17, 1969, the day after his father, Sanford Kahrmann, died at age 55. Peter was 15.

The Shed Of A Tear

This gigantic heart
Pumping moment pulls
Me joyous across
Enchanting smooth
Soft glimpses
And the shed of a tear

I cannot forgive
The tears in all
This thought movement
A clenching sadness
Yanks me
And the shed of a tear

The unavoidable missing
Sits me down still
With Sweaty Palms
For the unheard voice
In the morning
And the shed of a tear

And the gentle
Cast in daylight moment
And the rising to my feet
And the sweet hug
Melting me warm
And the shed of a tear
Home with No Name
Home with no name,
This charcoal deep airy lost place.
Cut bonds and cords flit in the wind,

a thousand tentacles.
Sad hearts stand in quiet corners,
lost, trembling,
cold, bent, buckled,
they weep – they weep.

Now, stumbled to standing,
I'll split the heavens for you,
snare the brightest sun.
Across the pond
out of reach
your heart glistens
warm gold love.
I am now,
finally,
bound by nothing
but me.
If I could only
cleave the pond in two,
and be lost no more.

Embrace

That someone would hold me
at the end
of day
I pray
boldly

Dancing Glory

Movements burst
Kaleidoscope flecks
Dancing to sunlight
Wide open full swirl
Spinning across the floor
O! the glory of dancing
Ineffable life your heart
Pumps your
Ode to joy

Feathered Highways

Dancing soft footed down feathered highways
Dreaming of my father mother where'd they go
My dancing rhythmic movements pleading
Hear me my call my heart my soul
Don't let the sundown past mountains
Beyond where silence absorbs
The scope of things
Silencing breath

In A Good Way

We look for the meaning now
Lamenting the Styrofoam embracing our coffee
And the young male teen who just walked
By talking tough like he knows strength
Someone saying - Like to teach the
Little shit a lesson

But they mean that in a good way

In hot vein moments we snarl jointly
At the Bosnia slaughter and I ask
What did we mean when we said never again
And minutes later coming home from
The day you pointed out a majestic tree and slowed
The truck in awe - never mind the screech behind us

I mean that in a good way.

And on the job, we crank to high standards
Your shuffling pace spots the missed nick
The unfinished sweep the ugly table we moved
To paint a room - muttering lit fuse quick
Before telling me, my sanded walls look good

You mean that in a good way

Then that phone talk and connection across
The landscape of ripped childhoods
With minds and hearts bleeding

To the bump and grind of abuse
And our little boys met and
I'm damn glad they did (I mean that in a good way)

Breathe

I'm saving my life
These days you listening?
I'm saving my life

Hope you'll hear my moment
Hope you'll hear my breath

Breathe

I am the anger sheathed
With no bullshit
The blistering wide open
It's my concrete scrape
It's my bent neck

Breathe

I am neck down blind
But for my child's face
Sifting into darkness
In the carved blood moment
the struggle wrenches full

I'm saving my life these days
I know that bullet
Cracked me open
I knew I was gone
I get it

Breathe

Words I've Written

In the words I have written
I have often
found myself caught
in the quandary of their power.
It is a simple thought
the will and wish to create.
Yet we must
as flawed mortals
devote ourselves to truth.
The mightiest task of all.
If in my life
I can divulge one solitary grain,
perhaps then I can die
in peace and sleep
throughout eternity
with a smile.

Joy

Joy
Like that morning cheek to belly press
The coffee smile tossed gently over
The top of reading glasses
Man, I'll tell you joy

Joy
When the chocolate covering
On the ice cream bar fractures
For the teeth just right
I'll tell you joy

Joy
The walking through the door moment
And your face is there
Pulling me warm home
Yeah, I'll tell you joy

Joy
Making the words carve
Me a new world on the soft
Side of a hill somewhere
I'll tell you joy (just told you mine)

Quick

Dreams pass me quickly
Sounds colors whirling
Do you hear me?

Curling through spring lit morns
Smooth tasting breast buttermilk rich

Do you hear me?

Hair like raven jewels
Eyes laced truth unfolding

Do you hear me?

Morning brings us hummingbirds
Our smokey voices whispering smiles

Do you hear me?

Kiss me quick!

It Was Your Heart I Wanted

In this hard stone granite loss moment
I hold close the words of my never
To be gone language until I am
Singing it was your heart I wanted
In the face of love fear driven knees
Buckle from history's wounds standing
On Ode to Joy's unflinching throne
Singing it was your heart I wanted
Casting a glance over my shoulder
I hold close the dream all gone
Grateful it whispered soft to me
It was your heart I wanted

Beyond Quiet

Here I am now silent quiet
before dark solitude thought
beyond beyond quiet
all in peace.

Sudden swerve away and again
I've placed thought before me
untouched in fetal posture
ignorance the victor again.

Swept up from beneath earth
father's memory against my face
steam pressed clasping complete
I cannot turn.

I see I hear you're moved closer
I hear you closer moved
eyes clamped shut clutching memory
soundless then know it.

Ponder not why life
is not stripped and pondered
and no asking why
betwixt how can i know

Were the ways within my grasp
to immerse full length in you...

For the Likes of This Lad

Stone bone weary sadness buckles my days stumbles my nights
No use dreaming like I just done did again never
Learning sunshine days visit but never stay
                    For the likes of this lad

Wounded hearts bleed from wounded souls starving still
Love's last chance offered by splayed finger hands breaking
The sweat stained life's killing habits leaves only darkness
                    For the likes of this lad

Warm sun mornings hint dreams worth dreaming
Muscled legs standing back straightens tears wiped clear
Birds sing jewels into the morning air joyous
                    For the likes of this lad

Leavin' no song unsung poem unread dream undreamed
Leavin' no hug, no kiss no touch unfelt
Leavin' no chance untried no love unloved no breath undrawn
                    For the likes of this lad

When The Words Are Gone

Hard drawn moments look
To shut me down and do
When the words are gone
Where is my father?
I am loosely tethered
To the life I'm in
When the words are gone
Where is my mother?

On A Distant Floor

Seen her sweat-shuffle moves down Main Street way sending
Smiles warm blasting hearts dizzy buckling knees she strides on
Seen her in a car just passing head spins sideways catching rainbows
Glancing sunlight ricochets off her eyes for me she drives on
Seen her skirt swirl as she turns dancing free of worries
On a distant floor in the world no more she moves on
Seen her in a dream last night smiling all the best made dreams
Woke up in the chill cold still of morning no lights on

All My Life

I am the blood cut word now
The slid back movement
On the run I am personified
Weariness muscle

I am the angered moment rising
The bare faced wonder
On the shifting page I am all
The borning letters

I am the powered legs striding
The inhaler of earth sounds
On my rhythmic runs I am
Freedom dancing music

I am the wound you want to know
Split-skulled and waiting in the safety
Of your home I am the road
You never traveled

I am muscled hills exploding color
The unbowed tear on a glorious
Day singing out I am
All my life now

Canted Dreams

Canted dreams edge the sky
Morning rain dimples ponder pond
He turns quick away the dream unfolds
Softly mourns the unspoken
Did you ever believe

His word set down strong
Bolted hard fast firm solid
All his stark stride moving
Slips past shadowed hopes
Did you ever believe

Buckle down mister boy
Shackled hearts histories abound
Silent vapor trails weave unheard
Hoped for rhythms all gone now
Did you ever believe

Heaven

With a slide slip thrust
Into your pulsing being
I am touching
Heaven

Time With Being

Is it all right
if I just am
for a moment?
(A humble request
by any measure.)
What is my life
if my time being
is left unspent?

Amatory Movement

She
turns words
loose in me
gentle soft travelers
sent across all of her
being in deep amatory
movement wandering
her sweet configurations
in velvet darkness
feather tasting
undulating shapes
I'd believe
unreal if
I wasn't
awake

Dancing With The Day

I do not fear the word
or experience sensual.
So much of life is.
Cool crisp
sweet-breezy
mornings tasty beings
all senses agree
these are our words
dancing with the day.

Cuddle

Per the droppers on the window
hinting the scent of wet leaves
good reading weather.
Cuddle.

Word Spun Fire

This may be not hard this word display
frankly you could say your word spun fire
into oblivion's vanishing blast.
I owe no lines across borders
none there are but nature's law's
wounding humanity.
This may be not hard this word display
frankly you could say your word spun fire
into oblivion's vanishing blast.
I owe no lines across borders
none there are but nature's law's
wounding humanity.

And The Tears Roar

And the tears roar punches down
Wetlands drenching twists
A muscled foe
Into spirit
Form

Violence

I am sick of violence. All kinds.
Physical. Emotional. Spiritual.
Financial. Environmental. Bigoted.
Your capacity to inflict violence
is not a measure of your strength.
Rubbish. Violence and strength,
nothing synonymous
about them.

Sky

Muscled thighs
churn muddy strides
up a steep hill
then another
one then
sky

Frenzy Soft Moments

It went from frenzy soft
Moments slipping deep into
Moisture warm sliding into
Each other's center
Losing track of where body
Moments began and ended
This salacious duet seizing
The moment whole
Their passion
Diving deep and deeper
Into each other's grasp
The walls of where
They were embraced
Fell full away into
Velvet warm black
Leaving the slippery glow
Of skin to skin sliding
In a creamy warm embrace
Their eyes puffy
In primal heart-soul rhythm
Her soft glistened wetness
Slid across his tongue dipping
Into her deeper tasting
Seed in feathered droplets
Across her lips
Drinking
Each other dry
As their souls
Embraced

Spit Shine

Let me spit shine some words for a ramble
on this page words my word rhythms
be set free they walk stride skip
carrying you along for how long
we've yet to see remember
to breathe now breathe
necessary you
know

Banning Cruelty

And then, finally, anger.
Not the pound-the-table
with your fist anger,
but the center of your soul
anger, provoked by cruelty,
anger known to lift
veils of denial, confusion,
doubt. Cruelty deserves
no presence in any life.
You betray no one
but you if you fail
to ban cruelty
from your life.